She'd never fo[rgotten that] day.

Not joyful with su[nshine, n]ot [ev]en angry with storms, [just gr]ey and overcast. Sullen. A man and a woman taking part in a ceremony not blatantly happy but prudently furtive, and left trapped in a marriage filled with guilt and resentment.

Terse

Dear Reader

This is the time of year when thoughts turn to sun, sand and the sea. This summer, Mills & Boon will bring you at least two of those elements in a duet of stories by popular authors Emma Darcy and Sandra Marton. Look out next month for our collection of two exciting, exotic and sensual desert romances, which bring Arab princes, lashings of sun and sand (and maybe even the odd oasis) right to your door!

The Editor

Catherine Spencer, once an English teacher, fell into writing through eavesdropping on a conversation about Harlequin romances. Within two months she changed careers and sold her first book to Mills & Boon in 1984. She moved to Canada from England thirty years ago and lives in Vancouver. She is married to a Canadian and has four grown children—two daughters and two sons—plus three dogs and a cat. In her spare time she plays the piano, collects antiques, and grows tropical shrubs.

Recent titles by the same author:

LADY BE MINE

LOVE'S STING

BY
CATHERINE SPENCER

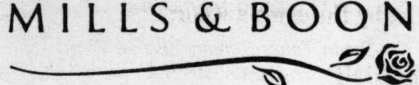

MILLS & BOON LIMITED
ETON HOUSE, 18-24 PARADISE ROAD
RICHMOND, SURREY TW9 1SR

> **DID YOU PURCHASE THIS BOOK WITHOUT A COVER?**
>
> If you did, you should be aware it is **stolen property** as it was reported *unsold and destroyed* by a retailer. Neither the Author nor the publisher has received any payment for this book.

All the characters in this book have no existence outside the imagination of the Author, and have no relation whatsoever to anyone bearing the same name or names. They are not even distantly inspired by any individual known or unknown to the Author, and all the incidents are pure invention.

All Rights Reserved. The text of this publication or any part thereof may not be reproduced or transmitted in any form or by any means, electronic or mechanical, including photocopying, recording, storage in an information retrieval system, or otherwise, without the written permission of the publisher.

This book is sold subject to the condition that it shall not, by way of trade or otherwise, be lent, resold, hired out or otherwise circulated without the prior consent of the publisher in any form of binding or cover other than that in which it is published and without a similar condition including this condition being imposed on the subsequent purchaser.

*MILLS & BOON and the Rose Device
are trademarks of the publisher.*

*First published in Great Britain 1994
by Mills & Boon Limited*

© Kathy Garner 1994

*Australian copyright 1994   Philippine copyright 1994
This edition 1994*

ISBN 0 263 78549 1

*Set in Times Roman 10½ on 12 pt.
01-9407-50497 C*

Made and printed in Great Britain

CHAPTER ONE

APART from herself, two distant cousins and the maid hired for the occasion, everyone else at the bridal tea was gathered in the reception rooms of the Dunns' gracious house. Busy admiring the latest wedding gifts, they didn't hear the hiss of the door swinging open, and remained blissfully ignorant of Sharon's return from the kitchen, cake tray of *petits fours* balanced on one hand. Which was probably why Miss Jubilee Bodine felt at liberty to give voice to words never intended for Sharon's ears.

'How long do you suppose we can keep the news from her that Our Boy is back in town?'

The meaning of her question was as unmistakable as the resonant whisper she'd developed since her hearing had started to fail. As far as the Bodine sisters were concerned, there was only one person on the face of the earth whom they referred to as 'Our Boy', and the fact that he must be thirty-eight by now didn't hinder them a bit.

He was the sun, moon and stars in their heaven, all rolled up into one. He was Clinton Bodine, their great-nephew, their adopted child, the light and life of their declining years. And he was Sharon's ex-husband, whom she'd hoped never to see again, least of all here in a town she'd thought he despised almost as much as he despised her.

'Hush, Jubilee!' Miss Celeste Bodine shook a finger and jerked her head towards the door at her back. 'Sharon might hear.'

But the warning came too late. From the other end of the dining-room, Margot looked up, saw Sharon, and groaned audibly. The chatter dribbled into silence. All eyes turned to discover the cause of the bride's distress and came to rest on Sharon, poised in the doorway, the *petits fours* in danger of sliding from their doilied silver platter to the polished oak floor.

Laden cake forks hovered at open jaws, a lapse of manners not normally countenanced in the refined social circles of Crescent Creek. Miss Celeste clapped a hand to her mouth. Miss Jubilee turned raspberry-red. Vera Dunn, the mother of the bride, continued to pour tea into a china cup, even though it was already full to overflowing. Margot's brown eyes widened in dismay, then lowered guiltily.

The only person not frozen with shock was Fern, who, in love with the importance of being a bridesmaid for the first time in her short, sweet life, continued to hum Wagner's 'Wedding March' and pace studiously back and forth on the terrace beyond the open French doors of the dining-room.

Among the adults, Sharon recovered first. 'What did you say, Miss Jubilee?'

'Sharon...!' Margot stuffed wafer-thin champagne flutes into their tissue-lined gift box with little regard for their fragility, and came towards her with hands outstretched.

'Darling girl!' Miss Celeste whimpered, horrified.

Miss Jubilee muttered, 'Eh?' and tried to look a little deafer than she really was.

Sharon stared her straight in the eye. 'Did I understand you correctly?' she asked, enunciating each syllable clearly. 'Did you say that Clint is in town?'

'Yes,' Miss Jubilee mumbled, paling rapidly.

'When did you learn he was coming back?'

The old lady stared down at her gnarled fingers and blinked. The silence took on a heavy, smothering air of foreboding that made it hard to breathe normally.

'Miss Jubilee?' Sharon prompted, a shade more gently. The old sweetie was eighty-two, after all.

'The... other day.'

'And when did he arrive?'

'Last night.'

Good grief; considering that only one flight a day landed at Crescent Creek's decrepit little airport, it was a miracle they hadn't bumped into each other before now!

'Sharon——' Margot tried again, a note of pleading in her voice.

Sharon silenced her with a slashing motion of her free hand. 'And when were you going to let me in on the news?'

Miss Jubilee's shoulders lifted helplessly. 'He asked us not to mention it to you.'

And of course, it had never occurred to either aunt to disregard his wishes. If Clint had ordered them to burn their house to the ground, they'd probably have done so.

Sharon swallowed an exasperated sigh. 'Why not? Don't you think, considering I was once married to him, that I had a right to know something that's obviously common knowledge to everyone else here?'

'Oh, dear!' Miss Celeste wrung her hands. 'Please, darling girl, don't let Clinton's presence spoil the wedding for you.'

Apprehension raced up Sharon's spine. 'How could it?' She swung her gaze to the bride, her friend since college days, the one person who knew why it was imperative that Clinton Bodine be kept as far away from Sharon as possible. 'He's not invited to the wedding—is he?'

Silence, except for Fern's absorbed humming.

'*Is he, Margot?*'

Margot dipped her head in shame.

The *petits fours* slid on to the floor then, and rolled under the table. 'Oh, dear heaven!' The words fluttered past the constriction in Sharon's chest, and all the prettily patterned dresses of the ladies merged into a blur of dizzying colour.

Someone took the silver platter from her hand. Someone else pressed her into a chair. Margot stroked her face. Miss Celeste urged her to sip tea.

'How *could* you?' Sharon whispered, pushing Margot away.

'I was going to tell you...I didn't know myself until...Sharon, what could I do? Tell him he wasn't allowed back in town?'

'I would have, in your place,' Sharon raged quietly. 'And you can bet your last miserable dollar he wouldn't be a guest at my wedding.'

'Alan wanted to invite him, and I could hardly refuse. It's his wedding too, after all.' Margot sighed unhappily. 'I had no choice.'

'Well, lucky for me, I do! I'm out of here, first thing tomorrow.'

Margot's wail brought all eyes swinging their way once more. 'I knew that's how you'd react! That's why I didn't want to tell you.'

'What else did you expect?' Sharon glared, deliberately fuelling her anger at the betrayal, because if she didn't she knew she'd collapse in a babbling heap of hysteria. Then everyone would know what she was trying so desperately to conceal: that it wasn't animosity or bitterness towards her ex-husband that left her in such a state; it was mortal fear.

'Darling girl,' Miss Celeste ventured, her sweet face crumpling, 'it's been ten years. Can't you forget and forgive?'

Not in this lifetime! Sharon thought miserably. To her dying day she'd remember the hunted look on Clint's face the day he'd stood before the marriage commissioner and repeated his wedding vows. And she'd never forgive the expression that had flared in his eyes when he'd learned that she'd miscarried the baby. A man granted a last-minute reprieve from the hangman's noose couldn't have appeared more relieved!

'For our sakes?' Miss Jubilee begged. 'We've seen him so seldom, ever since...'

'Please don't go,' Margot implored.

Never an easy woman, Vera Dunn was a dragon when crossed. She was crossed now. 'You can't go,' she declared in that bossy way that had always set Sharon's teeth on edge. 'I won't allow it.'

'Oh, yes, I can,' Sharon retorted.

'What, and disappoint your little daughter when she's been looking forward to this wedding for so long? Surely you wouldn't do that—not to mention letting down the rest of the wedding party? After all, Sharon, everything has been arranged for months, and the numbers simply won't add up if we lose our little bridesmaid.'

As though on cue, Fern pushed her way through the crowd and came to lean against Sharon's knee. She gazed at her with clear green eyes inherited, thank God, from her mother's side of the family. 'Mommy? Are you sick?'

Oh, yes! Sick to the soul. 'No, darling.'

'Your mother,' Mrs Dunn announced, pink-cheeked with annoyance, 'is thinking of taking you home and missing the wedding, Fern. What do you have to say about that?'

'My mommy won't do that,' Fern said with childlike certainty, and fixed trusting eyes on Sharon. 'She promised I could be a bridesmaid, and she never breaks her promises, do you, Mommy?'

Sharon slumped in the chair. 'Not if I can help it.'

'Good. Then it's settled.' Mrs Dunn brushed one palm against the other dismissively, as though to say that now that Sharon had had her little fit she should stop being tiresome and remember who really belonged in the limelight. 'Perhaps it's time we switched from tea to sherry. Margot, dear, why don't you pour Sharon's first? It might settle her nerves.'

'Sharon?' Margot hesitated uncertainly.

Sharon waved her away. 'Pour your own, and make it a stiff one. You're going to need it,' she promised, 'before I'm through with you, because the subject is not closed, Margot, not by a long shot.'

The bridal tea droned on interminably, the precursor not of a week of celebration, as Sharon had expected, but of prolonged stress and uncertainty. Cameras clicked; murmurs of approval hummed as gifts were handed around for inspection. Speculation arose about the honeymoon destination. Traditions were discussed as if their preservation were of cosmic importance: the wedding-dress was new, the heirloom pearls old, but what about something borrowed, something blue?

Sharon endured it all, veiling her agitation behind an air of tranquillity that fooled everyone but Margot. As soon as she could decently do so, she escaped into the garden and hid in the rose arbour, unable to put off a moment longer deciding how she was going to deal with the situation suddenly confronting her.

She could run away, of course. She had before, but then so had he, so no one had paid much attention. But if she were to go this time, abandoning her best friend and depriving her of one of the bridesmaids, just because a man she'd once been married to showed up, people would surely wonder. Wondering led to gossiping, which was only a hop away from conjecturing, and there was always the outside chance that someone would put two and two together and come up with four.

If that should happen, the repercussions would be disastrous, which left her with only one alternative. She had to stay, face Clint, and do whatever was required to protect her secret.

He'd never thought he'd live to see the day that Crescent Creek would look good to him. While the rest of the world grappled with war and upheaval, this town went steadily about its business, protected by a sort of time warp in which golf handicaps and soirées created the headlines, and poverty and corruption were relegated to the back pages, as befitted matters occurring elsewhere. The closest to political graft that anyone here had come was the time the ex-mayor used his influence to get his wife elected president of the horticultural society.

Clint stretched out in the hammock strung between two ancient copper beeches, folded his hands behind his head, and wondered how long it would be, in a town this size, before he and Sharon came face to face. An hour? A day?

One thing he knew for sure: he wasn't about to wait until the wedding to see her. Their first meeting in ten years was not going to take place before a crowd of gaping witnesses nodding wisely and whispering behind their hands as though they saw more happening than quite met the eye. It was going to be conducted privately, at a time and place of his choosing.

A very odd thing had happened on the afternoon he'd run into Alan Wilson during a four-hour stopover in Chicago's O'Hare Airport and learned of his old football mate's upcoming marriage to Margot Dunn, Sharon's best friend. Memories he'd sworn he'd successfully buried had suddenly risen up to confront him with shocking clarity, and he'd known at that moment that the running must come to an end.

It hadn't taken much interrogative skill to find out that Sharon was invited to the wedding. What *had* taken some doing was hiding his response to the information. Possessed by a burning curiosity to see again the woman he'd once promised to love and cherish, for better or worse, for the rest of his life, he'd wangled an invitation for himself out of the bridegroom, then rationalised his behaviour by telling himself that Fate had intervened and handed him a golden opportunity to lay the past to rest. There was no question but that he'd have to do that, if he seriously intended to abandon his vagabond ways and settle down peacefully in Crescent Creek.

The last thing he'd ever expected was that his and Sharon's paths would cross again, after all this time, in the same small town where they'd met. Would he recognise her? he wondered. She'd been nineteen the first time he'd seen her, and so bloody beautiful and self-assured that he'd been more than ready to believe her when she'd told him she was twenty-three. But that was ten years ago, and people changed... grew fat and sloppy.

The idea of Sharon growing fat or sloppy had him laughing out loud. A less likely candidate he could hardly imagine. When he'd met her she'd just won an apprenticeship with an Italian fashion designer and, according to Alan Wilson, she'd gone on to make quite a name for herself in the world of *haute couture*. She'd probably become cold and hard. In a cut-throat business like hers, it would be difficult not to, and she'd always been ambitious.

He stretched again, and closed his eyes, picturing the eager young woman she'd once been, so poised on the outside, so defenceless within. She'd been so young, had had such a zest for life. What drove her today? Success? Money?

It was good, he supposed, that she'd been able to forge ahead with her career, and male ego made him wonder if she'd ever regretted what she'd given up in return.

Disturbed from his afternoon nap at Clint's feet, Jasper, the aunts' overweight basset hound, flopped over the side of the hammock and waddled off around the side of the house, baying joyfully. The tidal wave of motion that resulted tipped Clint off, too, and tumbled him on to the grass. It needed cutting, he noticed, and made a mental note to take care of it later. Right now he had other obligations. Jasper's greeting signalled the return of the aunts, who'd no doubt be itching to regale him with details of the bridal tea.

It was just as well they were home. Too much lying around, swigging Celeste's home-brewed cider, could add inches to a man's waist without his even noticing. And Clint was damned if he was going to come face to face with Sharon after ten years to have her look him over pityingly and wonder aloud if he'd ever thought of going on a diet.

Slapping the flat of his hand against the ridged muscle of his stomach, he loped over the grass to the rear porch. Had she been at the tea, too? And if so, would his aunts volunteer the information, or would he have to weasel it out of them, a syllable at a time?

He wasn't left wondering too long.

'Oh, Clinton! The most awful thing happened at the tea,' Aunt Celeste panted, meeting him at the back door. 'Come and sit with us while Jubilee and I tell you about it.'

He slung an arm around her stooped shoulders and walked through the house with her to the cool, high-ceilinged living-room. 'You spilled tea on Mrs Dunn's silk carpet and she's having you burned at the stake.'

'Worse,' Aunt Jubilee confessed from the sofa, fanning herself with her hat. 'Sharon was there, and she knows. She overheard me talking about your being home for the wedding.'

Cursing inside, he smiled reassuringly and bent to help Celeste ease off shoes that were at least half a size too small for her feet. 'So?'

'She was terribly upset,' Celeste said. 'She threatened to leave town.'

'Tomorrow,' Jubilee put in gloomily. 'If the new airport at Harperville were open, she'd probably have gone tonight.'

But the Harperville airport wasn't due to open for another six months, and the next flight out of Crescent Creek didn't leave until noon tomorrow.

Clint made his plans for early the following morning.

After she'd dressed for dinner, Sharon slipped into the adjoining room and stood by the bed, watching her child with the same sense of wonder that had touched her the day she'd held her in her arms for the first time. Fern's dark blonde eyelashes lay long and thick on her cheek, her curled fingers snuggled beneath her chin. Her mouth, pursed sweetly in sleep, formed a perfect bee-sting.

'My miracle baby,' Sharon whispered, her heart so full that she thought it would burst. She turned away, stifling a sigh of regret for the wisdom of hindsight come much too late.

When Margot had asked her to design her trousseau and bridal ensemble, Sharon had been happy to comply, though she'd never intended actually coming to town for the wedding itself. But Margot had then complicated matters terribly by asking Fern to be a bridesmaid, and Sharon had been forced to admit to her friend that she was afraid to come back to Crescent Creek, a town that held few fond memories for her and more grief and regret than any person deserved in one lifetime.

'What if Clint chooses the same time to pay his aunts one of his infrequent visits?' she'd protested. 'Two hundred and twenty miles from Vancouver isn't that far off the beaten track for a world traveller like him, after all, and, although he professed to hate its small-town mentality, Crescent Creek *is* the only real home he's ever known, Margot.'

But Margot had pooh-poohed the notion. 'You're overreacting, Sharon. The last anyone heard of Clint, he was up to his neck shipping refugees from some country under siege in Eastern Europe—and that's about as far removed from here as he can get. And anyway,' she'd concluded with inimitable good sense, 'what do you think he'd do if, by chance, he did happen to show up? Corner you and insist you give him a blow-by-blow account of your every movement since the divorce? He probably wouldn't be interested and, even if he were, it's none of his business, as he'd be the first to admit.'

It had seemed a plausible argument at the time, and a risk worth taking for a friend who had remained constant through the best and worst days of Sharon's life. Returning the favour by agreeing to attend her wedding was an admittedly small price to pay for Margot's loyalty.

Someone tapped softly on Fern's bedroom door. 'Sharon?'

Margot's voice, almost timid with apprehension, left Sharon feeling ashamed. Mrs Dunn was right. She had no business spoiling this week for her friend, and no right to blame her for Clint's whereabouts or inclinations.

'Sharon?' Another light tap. 'Are you there?'

'I'm here.' Dropping a kiss on Fern's cheek, Sharon flung a silk shawl around her shoulders and opened the door.

'I thought we might talk—about what...' Margot's soft brown eyes pleaded for understanding.

'About Clint's being at the wedding,' Sharon finished for her. 'Look, Margie, I'm sorry if I took it out on you this afternoon, but I was——'

'Shocked. I know. So was I, when I first heard.'

'Actually, "flabbergasted" might be a better word. I'm afraid I reacted very badly. Your mother will never forgive me.'

'I won't forgive you, if you run out on me before my wedding!'

'I'm not going anywhere—at least not until I see you safely off on your honeymoon.'

'Oh, thank you!' Margot sagged against the door. 'I keep having the most awful attacks of wedding nerves, and you're the only one who'll keep me sane on the big day.'

'In that case, you can relax. I'm not the type to run away—not any more.'

It was true. She was no longer the nineteen-year-old pregnant wife of a man who felt as though he'd been hog-tied and forced into marriage; she was the successful widow of a man who'd loved her enough to accept her previous mistakes without once reproaching her for them. If Jason were alive today, he'd tell her to stand her ground. Clint Bodine had forfeited the right to dictate the terms by which she conducted her life.

Margot touched her hand in sympathy. 'I'm sorry you had to find out the way you did, with everybody listening in and watching.'

Sharon glanced at her sharply. 'Why? Did someone say something?'

'Nothing worth repeating or worrying about, and we're already late for dinner, so let's go down.' But although she sounded confident, Margot slewed her glance away and fixed it on the stairs.

It was a mannerism that Sharon knew well, and it caused a tremor of alarm to ripple over her. She grabbed at her friend's sleeve, preventing her escape. 'There's something you're not telling me. What is it?'

Margot chewed her lip, then shrugged. 'All right. People who knew you then think you're still a little in love with Clint. That you never really got over him.'

'Oh, please!' Relief had Sharon hiccuping with laughter as she started down the stairs. 'I got over Clint Bodine the day he walked out of our marriage. If I feel anything at all for him, it's gratitude. Thanks to him, I was free to marry Jason when he asked me.'

'If you say so,' Margot said placatingly.

Sharon clutched the banister and stared over her shoulder. 'For heaven's sake, Margie, my reasons for not wanting to see him again have nothing at all to do with left-over puppy love, as you of all people should know.'

'I suppose. But you were crazy about him, at the time.'

Crazy. It was a good word—the *only* word, in fact—to describe the inexcusable duplicity that had eventually led her to such heartbreak and grief. That she should be forced into another round of deceit now, when she'd thought herself safely past the need, infuriated Sharon beyond measure.

Checking to make sure no one was close enough to eavesdrop, Margot whispered, 'What about Fern?'

'What about her? Clint Bodine isn't interested in children. We both know that.'

'But what if he finds out?'

Hearing her own worst fears put into words threatened to unravel all of Sharon's tightly woven control. 'We can't let him, not after all this time. It would hurt too many people.'

'But what if he guesses?'

'Why should he? No one else has.'

Margot sighed unhappily. 'If only you'd told him the truth from the beginning... But you were so sure you knew what you were doing.'

'I was sure of a great many things then, and I wish I had one tenth the same confidence now.' The evening was balmy, but she pulled the shawl more snugly around her shoulders as though to ward off a chill. 'One thing I do know, though, is that honesty isn't always the best policy. Sometimes telling the truth does more harm than good, especially if it comes nearly ten years too late.'

'Hmm.' Margot sounded unconvinced. 'Does that mean you've already decided how you're going to handle seeing him again?'

With extreme care, the way a person might handle a time-bomb that came flying through the window without advance notice!

'Take him by surprise,' Sharon replied, allowing none of her trepidation to show. 'I'm going to pay a call on him, first thing tomorrow, and make it plain that I am not interested in rehashing the past, that I bear him no ill will, but that the less I see of him, the better. By some freak of coincidence we're both guests at your wedding, Margie; that's all. It starts and ends there.'

And she truly believed every word, because there wasn't a reason in the world to doubt it.

CHAPTER TWO

THE Bodine sisters' house sat at the top of a winding hill on the east bank of the river that gave Crescent Creek its name. The Dunns' house was situated on the west bank. Leaving Fern to help Margot arrange wedding gifts in the library, Sharon set off first thing the next morning, intent on only one thing: seeing to it that Clint Bodine understood her ground rules and agreed to abide by them without question or argument.

It was a still June morning, with laser beams of sunlight slicing between the branches of the trees and glowing softly on the banks of flowers that lined the curving driveway. Sharon was glad to be alone. The solitude calmed her nerves and gave her an opportunity to rehearse what she planned to say when she arrived at the Bodines' front door.

Her preoccupation, added to the fact that the sun slanted into her eyes when she rounded a bend in the drive, was probably why she didn't see him coming the other way until she'd walked practically into his arms. Maybe it was best that things happened like that, because if she'd realised sooner who he was she might have lost her nerve and run back the way she'd come. As it was, he spoke before she recognised him, by which time it was too late to worry about the wisdom of yesterday's decision, and she was left with no choice but to face the man she'd gladly have avoided for the rest of her life, had such an option been possible.

'Hello, dear heart,' he said, his voice just as she remembered it—sexy and slightly rough, like velvet rubbed the wrong way. 'Where are you racing off to at such an early hour?'

'Looking for you,' she said, so discombobulated by his use of the old familiar endearment that it never occurred to her to quibble about his right to question her or otherwise interfere in her business.

'Well, you've found me.' He held his hands palms up and, although the sun continued to dazzle her, she could tell from his tone that he was smiling. 'Here I am, in the flesh. What did you want to see me about?'

Very slowly, her brain cells filtered back to normality. 'I wanted to talk to you.'

'Really? I'm flattered—especially since word has it that you were ready to fly the coop rather than face me.'

'You were misinformed,' she said, with a trace of asperity.

Legs straddling the ground, he grinned down at her, not the least abashed by her disclaimer. 'Does that mean that you're thrilled to see me, and over the moon that we're both invited to the same wedding?'

'Before you get carried away with conceit,' she replied, slewing her gaze away, because everything about him spelled appeal at its masculine best, and she'd rather die than have him read the knowledge in her eyes, 'let's get two things straight. First, whether or not you're a guest at the wedding is immaterial to me; and second, I wasn't on my way to see you because I'm interested in any sort of social intercourse.'

'Not even for old times' sake?' He practically cooed the words at her.

'Least of all for old times' sake. Just the opposite, in fact, and I hope you'll be gentleman enough to agree to what I'm about to suggest.'

To the left of where they stood, a wrought-iron park bench marked the beginning of a path that branched off from the main driveway and meandered towards the riverbank. At her words, Clint sauntered over to it and flung himself down, arms spread-eagled along its back. 'Forgive me for saying so, but, as I recall, we seldom agreed on anything much in the past. What makes you think it'll be different this time?'

'I'd like to think we're both a bit more mature than we were back then.'

He slithered over to make space for her beside him, and patted the bench invitingly. 'Why don't we find out? Sit down, dear heart, and tell me what's on your mind.'

Not a chance, she thought. Keeping her distance was the only safe route to take when dealing with a man like Clint Bodine. 'I don't think that's a very good idea.'

'Why not?' He grinned lazily at her, and crossed his long legs at the ankles, obviously enjoying her discomposure. 'Still ashamed to be seen with me?'

'I was never ashamed to be seen with you,' she shot back, 'so don't go making things worse than they really were.'

'I didn't think they could be made any worse,' he replied, sobering. 'I'd have said, if you'd bothered to ask, that we'd hit the skids with a vengeance by the time we decided to call it quits and go our separate ways.'

In the distance Sharon heard the slam of a door, followed, a second later, by a car's engine roaring into life. With a stab of alarm, she remembered that when they'd finished arranging the gifts Margot and Fern were driving into town to attend to some last-minute wedding chores.

Controlling the urge to dive for cover behind the trunk of a grand old Ponderosa pine, Sharon gestured towards the glimmer of water just visible beyond a dip in the path. 'Do you suppose we could walk down by the river? I feel foolish standing here, holding this conversation where anyone might see us.'

'You *are* ashamed,' he drawled, but rose to his feet with that same lithe and sexy grace that had contributed to her undoing ten years earlier. 'Either that, or you're afraid. Why, Sharon?'

'I'm past the age where I have to explain myself,' she snapped, so eager to put as much distance as possible between herself and any passing traffic that she would have tripped headlong over an exposed root had Clint not loped past her and caught her.

'And how old do you tell people you are these days, my dear?' he enquired smoothly, guiding her down the last steep stretch of bank to the curve of white sand edging the river.

His hands were capable and sure, darkly tanned against her milk-pale skin. Instruments of proficiency in work, she suspected, and of consummate skill in love, as she very well knew. She wrenched herself free, a flush derived equally from embarrassment and anger sweeping over her face. 'You've never forgiven me for that, have you?'

He shrugged, as though he couldn't be bothered expending the energy required to forgive her anything.

Feeling compelled to defend her past behaviour, she went on, 'Women have lied about their age for centuries.'

'Indeed they have,' he returned, 'but usually because they want to pass themselves off as younger, not older.'

'I fail to see how it makes much difference either way.'

He shook his head reproachfully, disturbing his neatly barbered hair. It was as thick as ever, she noticed, but there were strands of silver interwoven with the blond.

He was older, this one-time idol of hers. Always a handsome man—it was his male beauty, after all, that had caught her eye to begin with—he had, if it was possible, improved with age. The years had graced his features with a maturity that reflected the core of integrity that was perhaps his most admirable trait. The passion that shaped his mouth had become tempered by restraint, the arrogance in his eyes softened by humility.

'I think you know that it does,' he said, 'especially when the deceit results in such far-reaching consequences. I think you know that I would never have made love to you had I known you were only——'

'Made love?' She rounded on him, glad of an excuse to divert her thoughts. 'You seduced me!'

'No more than you seduced me,' he said.

Good grief, he was making her feel ashamed all over again! She pursed her lips disapprovingly and waged silent war on memories that insisted on springing to life in glorious Technicolor. 'This is one of the things I wanted to talk to you about.'

His lazy smile washed over her. 'What? Seducing me?'

He was impossible, and so busy exercising his charming side that it was hard to believe he was capable of chilling distance when roused to anger. 'We can hardly avoid seeing each other at the wedding,' she said coldly.

'Hardly,' he murmured, apparently fascinated by the collar of her blouse.

The buttons couldn't possibly have come undone during her scramble down the path, could they? 'I was hoping,' she continued, surreptitiously checking to make sure she was decent, 'that on those occasions when we can't avoid each other we could try to behave like civilised people and agree not to rake up the past. It's over and done with, and I find it frankly painful to rehash mistakes that can't be rectified.'

He switched his attention to her face and looked at her long and soberly, his gaze so potent that she quailed inside. 'And the others?'

'What?' Disconcerted by the dark, impenetrable blue of his eyes, she fumbled to make sense of his question.

'You said that was one of the things you wanted to talk about. What are the others?'

'Oh, yes.' Dismayed to find herself on the brink of regret for things she couldn't possibly change at this late date, she took a deep breath and stepped backwards, as though doing so might release her from his magnetic force field. 'I don't wish to be unpleasant, nor do I want to do anything to spoil this special time for Margot, but the simple fact of the matter is that you and I mean nothing to each other any longer. The way I see it, we're merely distant acquaintances, under no obligation to pretend an interest in each other that neither of us really feels.'

She knew she sounded about as engaging as a snarling wolverine, but what hurt was realising that he agreed with the estimation. The warmth fled from his gaze and he looked her over very thoroughly, as though she were a particularly repulsive specimen, but all he said was, 'I see.'

'Naturally I wouldn't dream of making a scene if we find ourselves thrown together by accident.'

'Naturally not.'

'I mean,' she continued, all the while wondering why she didn't just keep her mouth shut, since nothing she was saying was coming out right, 'there's been a lot of water under the bridge since...then.'

'Yes,' he said gravely. 'I understand you married again, since...then. Rather quickly, too.'

She stiffened. Was he taunting her? Implying that her true vocation was snagging husbands in quick succession by whatever means presented itself?

Deciding she didn't care, she traded level stares. 'Within a few short months, as a matter of fact.'

So what if he thought she'd rushed out with a net and trapped Jason before the ink had properly dried on her divorce papers? Perhaps it was better that way. It left less room for speculation or doubt. And Fern, thank God, had always been small for her age.

'But you've been widowed for some time?'

'Almost two years.'

'I'm sorry. Was it a good marriage?'

'The best. Based on all the right things.'

Not a vestige of emotion crossed his features. 'I see.'

'Like love,' she said, a trifle unhinged by his utter stillness, 'and respect. Admiration and liking.'

'What about sex?'

His audacity slammed her in the midriff and knocked the breath out of her. Caught off guard, she gaped and swallowed like an overwrought goldfish... and fought to recover herself. 'That too, of course.'

'Children?'

There it was, the question she *had* expected, and had thought herself prepared for. But she found herself shaking inside all over again. Her pulse shot into high gear, and fine beads of perspiration sprang down the length of her spine. 'One,' she managed, over the roaring pound of her heart.

He studied her for a long, quiet moment. Then, 'I'm glad,' he said at last. 'I'm sure that must have helped erase the bad memories left behind by our marriage.'

'It did,' she said defiantly. But the bad memories weren't what filled her mind as her eyes roamed over his tall, elegant frame. All she could recall was the breathless wonder of falling in love with him, and, try as she might, she couldn't conjure up Jason's dear face to rescue her. The sadness lurking in Clint's eyes got in the way.

Suddenly she saw not a man who'd run off to a life of high adventure, but someone who'd known more than his fair share of misery. If she'd lived with doubt and loneliness, he'd seen hell and lived to tell about it. What if she wasn't the only one who'd suffered, merely the only one who'd found consolation?

She smothered a sigh and wished she could hate him. And found herself instead lost in the mists of yesterday, her animosity softening into nostalgia, her reason battered by a surprising rush of desire.

He cleared his throat, as if he'd reached some sort of decision, and she found she was holding her breath, waiting to hear what was coming next. She had to keep her head, had to steer the conversation away from Fern. Anything, even having her heart broken a second time, was better than his suspecting that Fern——

'I'm sure,' he said, 'that it will take a load off your mind to hear that I agree entirely with most of what you've said. I'm too busy looking forward to the future to have any inclination to delve into the past. As far as I'm concerned, you're just another guest at a friend's wedding, and I'll treat you as such. No better, no worse.'

'Thank you. That's what I was hoping for.'

But if that were true, why did she feel as flat as yesterday's champagne, hollow inside, as if she'd just lost a battle, when, in fact, she'd won a major victory?

'See you at the wedding, then.'

'Yes.' It was relief, she told herself, that made her voice quaver like that, and almost reduced her to silly tears. She turned away, hoping he hadn't noticed, but she'd forgotten how observant he was.

'Sharon?' He moved dangerously close. 'Are you crying?'

What was the use of denying it, when her eyes were swimming and she could barely see enough to put one foot in front of the other? 'A little, I guess. First love is so painful, even in retrospect.'

'That's why it so seldom lasts,' he said, and reached out a finger as though to dam the tears that hovered on her eyelashes.

She couldn't endure to have him touch her. He was as potently, dangerously attractive as ever, if not more so. Raw with emotions she didn't pretend to understand, she flinched away from him. 'Go away and leave me alone,' she begged.

He backed off and held up both hands in surrender. 'Whatever you say, Sharon.'

His gentleness completely undid her. Instead of escaping with the dignity befitting a woman of almost thirty, she spun around and bolted back the way she'd come, leaving him standing there open-mouthed, no doubt, and wondering if she'd become completely unhinged.

In a way she had, because, appalling as it might be, the fact was she felt as bereft and desolate as she had the day they'd agreed to end their marriage. She couldn't bear to be the one left to watch him walk away again.

'Run as fast as you like, dear heart,' Clint said in soft response to her fading footsteps. 'It won't do you a bit of good.'

Exhaling a long, thoughtful breath, he narrowed his gaze against the glare of sunlight on the river. So, the future wasn't as uncomplicated as he'd thought, after all. No matter. He was used to change, and had plenty of practice adjusting to the unexpected.

He smiled and shook his head ruefully. She'd had him fooled at first, with that tough, lacquered approach. He'd been almost ready to believe what she said and consign her permanently to the past. But he was a man who'd learned to look beyond the obvious and, most of all, to trust his instincts.

He'd seen the way her pulse had raced so agitatedly that it set the open collar of her blouse fluttering. He'd seen how she'd nervously twisted the wedding-ring on her finger. But most of all, he'd seen the fear.

It had been there in her lovely green eyes from the minute she'd almost bumped into him on the drive. There'd been other emotions, too: shock, anger—her glare at his question about her sex life could have turned a man to stone!—and, once, regret, perhaps, and a certain wistful longing. But most of all, there'd been fear.

He knew why he'd deliberately engineered an invitation to the wedding. What he couldn't explain was her panic-stricken reaction to that unremarkable item of news. Was she afraid of him? Or herself?

He didn't know—yet. But he intended to find out, no matter how many barriers she threw up in an effort to deflect him.

The following afternoon the bridal outfits arrived by air courier, and wedding fever in the Dunn household escalated to new heights. Sharon found herself on permanent call, 'Because,' as Mrs Dunn pointed out almost every time she drew breath, 'things must be absolutely perfect.'

Sharon didn't mind being virtually house-bound and spending the next two days in the library, with no time for anything but making last-minute adjustments to hems and suchlike. She thought it would keep her safe from Clint.

She thought wrong. On the third day, with the bridesmaids' outfits at last pronounced acceptable, she came down to lunch with Fern to find him at the other side of the terrace, looking very much at home.

'Clint brought over his aunts' silver epergne,' Margot explained, shooting anxious glances back and forth between him and Sharon. 'Mother's borrowing it for the centrepiece at the reception.'

'I see,' Sharon said with what she hoped was convincing indifference. But what she saw was the way he smiled at Fern, who, accosted by a fit of shyness, half hid behind Sharon.

'So Mother invited him to stay for lunch,' Margot said.

She would! Sharon thought, her heart sinking as he strolled towards her with negligent, unhurried grace. Unobtrusively she reached behind and took Fern's hand in hers.

'Hi,' he said. 'How's it going?'

'Fine.'

'How does the wedding-dress look?'

'Fine.'

'And the bridesmaids'?'

'Fine.'

His eyes teased her unmercifully. 'How about having dinner with me tonight, then driving out to Crescent Point and watching the moon rise?'

Her heart tripped into overtime. The first time they'd made love had been at Crescent Point, with nothing but the rising moon to witness the event. 'Forget it,' she said shortly.

He grinned with unabashed glee. 'For a moment there, I thought you were going to say "Fine" again!'

'Was there something important you wanted to say?' she enquired. 'Or did you just come over here to see how quickly you could annoy me?'

'I was hoping you'd introduce me to this lovely young lady.'

Sharon's heart almost stopped at that, and she stared at him wordlessly, searching for an excuse not to do as he asked. She didn't want him talking to Fern; she didn't want him near her.

But he wasn't about to be put off. 'Sharon?'

'This is my daughter, Fern,' she said stiffly, and tensed, dreading that some eerie, latent intuition might tell him that Fern was his daughter, too.

'How do you do, Fern?' He bent down and enveloped her small hand in his with deferential charm. 'I'm Clint.'

Fern, Sharon noted with dismay, was no more immune to his charm than any other female. She gave him her hand, returned his smile, and murmured hello.

'Are you involved in this wedding, too?' he asked.

'I'm a bridesmaid,' she informed him pridefully.

'The prettiest, I'm sure.'

Fern giggled, falling more securely under his spell, and all Sharon could do was watch helplessly and pray that she could intervene before untold damage occurred. 'It's time to sit down, Fern,' she said, noting with heartfelt gratitude that Mrs Dunn was ushering people inside to the dining-room. 'Come along.'

'Will you save me a dance at the reception?' Clint asked his pint-sized conquest.

Fern released another endearing giggle. 'I don't know how to dance.'

'Neither do I,' Clint admitted, 'but I promise not to step on your toes if you promise not to step on mine.'

I'll break your leg first, Sharon thought balefully. He wasn't going to dance his way into her daughter's heart if she had any say in the matter.

But her ill-wishing fell on Mark, one of the ushers, instead, as she and everyone else learned when the bridegroom showed up halfway through lunch.

'Mark fell and broke his leg water-skiing on the river,' Alan explained. 'I'm afraid he won't be able to make it to the wedding.'

'Not make it to the wedding? But the numbers won't add up!' Mrs Dunn wailed, cutting through everyone else's exclamations of sympathy and getting right to the heart of what really mattered. 'Whatever are we going to do?'

'Fire a bridesmaid?' Alan suggested, attempting to lighten the atmosphere a little.

But while almost everyone else laughed, Mrs Dunn's glance roamed around the table and zeroed in on Fern. 'But of course!' she said. 'It's the perfect solution.'

'I was joking,' Alan protested, as the laughter settled into uneasy silence.

'It's no joking matter,' she declared. 'Fern will have to drop out.'

'Mother!' Margot half rose from her chair. 'You can't be serious.'

'Sharon never really wanted her involved to begin with,' Mrs Dunn said dismissively. 'Isn't that right, Sharon?'

Aware of Fern's strangled gasp of disappointment, Sharon fought to contain her anger at the woman's insensitivity. 'Not at all, Mrs Dunn. We both considered it an honour that she was invited.'

'Phooey! You were all set to rush back to Vancouver the day you heard Clinton was back in town, so don't pretend you weren't.'

'But I decided to stay,' Sharon replied, annoyed that such a juicy little morsel of information had been dropped almost literally on Clint's plate. 'And, if you recall, my reason for doing so was that I didn't want to disappoint Fern.'

Clint, who was seated on the other side of Margot, leaned behind her to exchange a few quick words with her fiancé. The other lunch guests pretended to be interested in the food on their plates, but the atmosphere was fraught with incipient hostility.

Mrs Dunn either didn't notice or didn't care. 'She'll get over it.' She shrugged.

'She won't have to,' Clint announced, concluding his muttered exchange with Alan. 'I'll stand in for the missing usher.'

'No, you won't,' Mrs Dunn snapped. 'You're at least three inches taller than he is. The rented suit won't fit.'

'Then we'll find one that does,' Clint said, overruling her with a smile that left his eyes flinty-cold.

Mottled with rage, Mrs Dunn glared the length of the table. 'This isn't your decision to make, Clinton.'

He usurped her authority with an unimpeachable courtesy that nevertheless brooked no opposition. 'Nor is it yours, Mrs Dunn. Selection of the ushers is the bridegroom's prerogative, a point of etiquette I'm sure you wouldn't dream of contravening, and Alan just accepted my offer to act as Mark's substitute.' The chill melted from his eyes as he shifted his attention to Fern. 'And that means I get to walk the prettiest bridesmaid down the aisle during the recessional,' he declared, increasing the wattage of his smile endearingly. 'I call that a lucky break—for me.'

Just about everyone laughed again at that, and Fern positively glowed with pleasure. But Sharon sat immobilised with horror, regretting that she hadn't acquiesced to Mrs Dunn's high-handed request before Clint opened his mouth and unwittingly trapped her more thoroughly in a web of complications that threatened to grow more tangled with every passing hour.

CHAPTER THREE

IN the well-mannered way that friends of the Dunns always behaved, people began talking about other things and pretended the rather acerbic exchange between hostess and guests had never occurred. Still not an ideal situation, it was nevertheless an improvement over the previous few minutes, and, glad for the reprieve, Sharon sat back and breathed a sigh of relief. Much too soon, as it turned out.

'What with everything else that's happening this week, I'd forgotten that the fair opens today,' Alan remarked. 'I could hear the noise when I drove by the park.'

Sharon didn't need Clint's penetrating stare to remind her that they'd met at Crescent Creek's annual country fair ten summers ago. The mere mention of it was enough to conjure up the memories with dismaying clarity. The sultry heat, the aroma of frying onions and home-made fudge mingling with the smell of diesel oil, the shrieks of terrified glee rising over honky-tonk music blaring from loudspeakers and underscored by the rumble of heavy machinery—it all came back with an immediacy that stunned her.

'Fair? What sort of fair?' Fern, who'd been slumped in her seat with boredom, perked up at Alan's disclosure.

'Don't tell me your mother hasn't mentioned it,' Clint said, his attempt to look guileless foiled by the secretive little smile that crept across his face. 'It's one of the high events of the summer in these parts. All sorts of interesting things have been known to happen during country fair week.'

Hadn't they, though? If she hadn't accepted Margot's challenge to risk her life on some crazy, gravity-defying machine that had left her too giddy to see where she was walking, Sharon might never have stumbled blindly into Clint Bodine's waiting arms. Then he'd have had no reason to cushion her next to his chest, or to suggest, in his smoky, alluring voice, that it might be wiser if he supervised any other rides she planned to try that long-ago day. But, at nineteen, she'd been too foolish to walk away from a dare, and as a result the course of her life and Clint's had been changed for ever.

'Are there merry-go-rounds and stuff?' Oblivious to the nuances of his comment, Fern regarded him from wide, hopeful eyes, and Sharon's heart sank. At the best of times, her daughter was appealing; right then, she was downright irresistible.

Clint, apparently, was no more immune than the rest of the world. 'You bet,' he assured her, abandoning his covert attack on Sharon and devoting all his attention to her daughter. 'Everything from carousels and Ferris wheels to ponies.'

'I've never ridden a pony,' Fern lamented.

'What?' He rounded on Sharon in mock-dismay. 'What sort of mother are you, Sharon, that your little girl's never ridden a pony?'

'There aren't too many horses running loose on Vancouver streets,' Sharon pointed out shortly, and wondered why in the name of sweet sanity she resented his being able to switch off *his* memories so easily.

'Then it's a good thing I can do something to rectify a very serious situation.' He angled an engaging smile Fern's way, captivating her completely. 'Miss McClure, will you allow me to escort you to the country fair and treat you to a ride on the ponies?'

He was as silver-tongued as ever, except this time it was his daughter he was disarming with his smile and his lazy, husky voice. Sharon wished he'd choke on all those perfect, dazzling teeth. Much as she'd like to see Fern having fun, she wasn't about to let Clint Bodine be the one to provide it.

Scraping her chair across the mirrored polish of Mrs Dunn's oak floor, she stood up and held out a hand to Fern. 'That's impossible. We're very busy between now and the wedding.'

Mesmerised by her new ally, Fern gazed at Clint adoringly. 'I'm not busy, Mommy,' she objected, adding with an adult logic that left Sharon at a loss for a suitable reply, 'In fact I don't have anything important to do until the wedding-day, and I'm quite bored.'

'I'll find something for you to do,' Sharon replied, a marked edge in her voice.

'There's no need for that,' Clint said mildly. 'I've already offered to take her off your hands for the afternoon. She'll be perfectly safe with me.'

'No.' Aware that almost everyone else at the table must think her a cold-blooded witch to remain unmoved by such monumental charm, Sharon turned her back on them all and swept Fern through the French doors and out into the garden.

Undeterred, Clint followed. 'You really shouldn't vent your hostility towards me by punishing your daughter,' he chided in a low voice.

'I'm not.'

'Then why won't you let me take her to the fair?'

'Because, in this day and age, smart parents don't send their children off with strangers. And stop interfering in the way I choose to bring up my own child.'

'I'm not a stranger.'

No, you're her father, but you don't know it; that's the whole trouble! 'Nevertheless...'

His gaze swept over her face, those brilliant, winsome blue eyes examining her feature by feature. 'What are you afraid of, Sharon? That I've turned into some sort of disgusting pervert who can't be allowed around innocent children?'

'Of course not!' But she was grievously afraid that if he ever found out how she'd deceived him he'd exact a terrible revenge.

'Then what's making you so antsy? And don't tell me I'm imagining things, because we both know better.'

He was too perceptive by half, and she much too transparent in her anxiety. 'I suppose it's just that I've become a bit over-protective ever since Jason died,' she parried, struggling to contain the panic that, left unchecked, might prove her undoing. 'Being a single parent is a great responsibility.'

'I can imagine that it must be.'

Perhaps so, but what he couldn't possibly imagine was the relief she felt at just once being able to open her mouth and state a simple fact, untarnished by evasions or half-truths. 'Then surely you can understand why I'm reluctant to let her go off without me?'

'Come with us and you won't have to deal with the problem.'

'I don't think...' Still trapped in his gaze, she searched for an excuse and instead found her thoughts veering again to the first time she'd seen him. He'd been tanned then, too, and his eyes had seemed as deeply blue as tropical seas. She'd floundered into their depths and into love within the space of a heartbeat.

'Come on, Sharon,' he cajoled her now. 'There's been a lot of water under the bridge since we decided to go our separate ways. Give me a chance to show you that I'm not a total jerk. Your little girl is hanging around with nothing to do. *You're* at the beck and call of Margot's mother as if you were a hired hand. Take the afternoon off and come with us to the fair.'

She couldn't afford to divulge the best reason in the world to refuse him. Worse yet, she wanted to go with him. It did no good to tell herself she was flirting with disaster, that the more time she spent around Clint, the greater the danger that he'd uncover her secret. Her heart overrode her head as easily now as it had ten years ago, luring her into dangerous waters without regard for her survival.

As if she'd been primed, Fern dealt a final blow to her resistance. 'Please, Mommy. I promise to be good.'

The child was always good; that was half the problem. She was the best thing that had ever happened to Sharon, the one person who made all the lies and sacrifices worth while. Disappointing her daughter was never easy. Her own imprudent inclinations aside, the guilt of knowing she'd neglected Fern over the last few days made it impossible for Sharon to refuse her now. 'Well, I suppose I could take a couple of hours...'

Something was very wrong. He grew surer of it by the minute. Even on the crowded fairground, with so much noise and activity going on that it was difficult to hear what the other person was saying, Sharon edged away from him as if he had typhoid or something. She even refused to look at him directly, though that could, perhaps, be explained by the fact that her gaze never wavered far from her daughter.

'She's safe for the next five minutes, Mother,' he teased at one point, as Fern rode the children's carousel. 'You can relax and start enjoying yourself.' And just to put his theory to the test, he cupped an impersonally friendly hand around her elbow.

Sure enough, she jumped and shied away as if he'd touched some intensely private part of her. What did she think? That he was such a depraved animal that he might toss her down behind one of the tents and have his way with her?

'This might come as a shock to you, dear heart,' he said mildly, 'but my intention in asking you to come with us this afternoon was not to terrorise you.'

'It never occurred to me that it was,' she said, then put the lie to her assertion by adding another twelve inches between them. It shouldn't surprise him; she'd lied to him before, after all.

The carousel slowed. From her perch on a painted unicorn, Fern waved happily. 'Do you hate me, Sharon?' Clint couldn't help asking.

She shot him an oblique glance from beneath long dark lashes. 'Why should I?'

Let me count the ways! he thought ruefully. 'You once told me that I'd ruined your life. The way you're acting now, I'm inclined to believe you think I'm still doing it.'

'All that happened a long time ago, Clint, and, as you eventually learned to our mutual cost, I was very young.'

'There are some things that time can't change or heal,' he said, wishing to hell he could come up with a more original reply. But he'd never been able to find the right words to make what had happened between them seem less painful. They'd lost their baby, and what remained of their marriage after that had been of so little substance that neither of them could find comfort in it.

As though she'd divined his thoughts, Sharon spoke again. 'You forget that I found Jason. I made a new life for myself after you left me.'

She made it sound like an accusation. 'You say that as if I walked out on you,' he said.

'You did, and it was the kindest thing you could have done. I would never have met Jason otherwise.'

A sudden anger caught him by surprise. This wasn't about Jason, it was about them, and he wasn't going to let her shift the focus to a man who had no part of their history. 'I don't give a flying fig about Jason, Sharon! And I did not leave you or walk out; we . . .'

But she moved out of earshot, intent on finding Fern, who'd hopped off the far side of the merry-go-round, a hazardous twenty-five yards away from her mother's vigilant surveillance.

'Where did Mommy go?' Breathless, Fern rushed around to him from the opposite direction, full of exuberance and glee, the way *their* child might have, had things gone differently. Come to think about it, the two children would have been about the same age, give or take a few months. Sharon must have conceived within hours of marrying good old Jason. Clint couldn't believe how much the knowledge soured his mood.

'Mr Bodine? Are you sad?'

It was impossible to remain surly in the face of such a sympathetic audience. He drummed up a smile. 'What makes you think that?'

'You looked a long way off and you didn't answer my question,' she replied, adding with artless candour, 'Mommy does that, sometimes, and it's usually because she's feeling sad.'

'Well, in my case, it's just that I wish you'd call me Clint instead of Mr Bodine. You are my date at the wedding, after all, so I think it would be OK—unless, of course, you'd rather keep things formal and have me call you "Miss McClure" all the time.'

She giggled, a light musical sound that enchanted him. 'I'm too young for that, but it's different with you. You're quite old.'

'Gee, thanks!' His laugh had Sharon scurrying back towards them. 'Here comes Mom,' he said. 'She went looking for you, but you fooled her and came around the other way. What do you want to do next?'

'The ponies,' Fern begged, appealing to him with huge green eyes so much like Sharon's that his heart faltered for a minute. 'Then the Ferris wheel—but only if you go on it with me. I'd be scared by myself.'

'It's a deal. The Ferris wheel is my favourite.'

'No!' Overhearing, Sharon practically arm-wrestled the child away from him, her voice unnaturally shrill. Even she seemed to realise she was overreacting, because she added lamely, 'She might get sick or something.'

'Pigs might fly,' he returned, 'but it isn't very likely.'

He recognised the stubborn set of her mouth and knew she was determined to oppose him even on so insignificant a point as this. 'Nevertheless, I think we should walk around the exhibits for a while, just in case,' she insisted.

'The exhibits are boring.' Fern pouted.

'Then we can go home,' Sharon said. 'I'd find that a perfectly acceptable alternative.'

The child was smarter than he by a country mile. Instead of fighting the issue, she switched tactics and favoured her mother with the sunniest of smiles. 'Some of them are boring,' she amended, 'but most of them are fun.'

Clint nodded towards a huge striped tent on the far side of the park. 'My aunts have a table in the country kitchen,' he told Sharon. 'They're selling home-made preserves and jams, and raffling off the patchwork quilt they made last winter. I know they'd love to have you stop by and visit.'

Just briefly a spark of interest gleamed, before the shutters rolled down over her beautiful eyes again. 'I don't think so, thanks.'

'They're harmless old ladies, Sharon,' he muttered, stifling the surge of annoyance that rose up in him. 'They have no part of your determined resentment of me.'

'It's not that.'

'Then why don't you tell what it is?'

'Fern,' she said, appearing to shuffle through half a dozen excuses before finding one that might hold water. 'I really can see that she might find jams and preserves a bit dull.'

'No problem,' he said easily. 'I'll keep her entertained for ten minutes while you go in and say hello. We'll stay here at the rifle shoot, where I'll do my damnedest to win her a doll or something, and I promise we won't move an inch until you come back.'

'A teddy bear!' Excitement at his suggestion had the child hopping around on one foot like a drunk on a pogo stick. 'A girl in my class has forty-two teddy bears, but I only have eight.'

'Holy cow!'

'Collecting bears is the latest rage among her friends,' Sharon explained, a near-smile softening her mouth at his astonished reaction to Fern's disclosure.

'Then a teddy bear is what I'll aim for, and she can be my cheering section. Go visit the aunts with an easy mind, dear heart.'

'Please don't call me that,' she muttered. 'Fern might hear and ask questions.'

'She'd have to have radar traps for ears to hear in this noise, but would it be so terrible if she found out that we were once married? That there was a time when——?'

Sharon looked aghast. 'Yes!' she hissed. 'She has no idea that... She thinks Jason...'

It was there in her eyes again, that flash of naked fear out of all proportion to the occasion. She reminded him of a doe trying to guard her fawn from hidden danger, and he felt alarmingly protective towards both of them, all of a sudden.

'I wish,' he said, 'that you trusted me enough to tell me what it is about my being here that's really bothering you. You'd have a far better time tomorrow night then, not to mention on the wedding-day itself.'

'Tomorrow night?' Her eyes flickered, seeking a way out of whatever mess she perceived herself to be in.

Confide in me, damn it!

Frustration had him wanting to shake some sense into her. Good God, had he left behind such a bad taste that she viewed him as some sort of monster, incapable of sympathetic understanding? 'The rehearsal dinner,' he reminded her, forcing himself to adopt a moderate tone. 'We're doomed to spend the evening together, whether you like it or not, and I venture to suggest it might be easier on both of us if we cleared the air first.'

'Are you going to win me a teddy bear?' Fern hopped back within hearing range, twitching with impatience, and Sharon seized the opportunity to deflect her attention away from him.

At first inclined to pursue the conversation with Sharon, Clint changed his mind and shrugged in defeat. 'If it's OK with your mom.'

'All right,' Sharon conceded, but reluctantly, as though he'd demanded a king's ransom in exchange for not hounding her. 'But I'd like to watch, if that's all right with you. I'll pay your aunts a visit later.'

His glance fell on the child at her side, and he knew a sharp pang of envy, mixed with an irrational anger, that Sharon had supplanted her loss with another man's child, while he had roamed the earth searching without success for an end to pain and for absolution of his sins. 'Whatever you say,' he acknowledged resignedly. 'She's your daughter, not mine, and you've already made it clear that you call the shots.'

She'd made a gross miscalculation when she'd decided she could handle seeing Clint again. It wasn't nearly as simple and nothing like as uncomplicated as she'd foolishly allowed herself to believe it would be. For a start, he'd changed. The old appeal was still there, possibly more potent than ever, but there was an added dimension Sharon hadn't counted on. No longer the kind who'd walk away from difficulties, he'd grown into a man who stayed with a problem until he'd resolved it, and the realisation petrified her. There was steel underneath all that charm, and she wasn't at all sure she could deflect its determined sense of purpose.

As for the rehearsal dinner, good lord, wasn't it enough that she had to endure the entire wedding-day with him hovering over Fern, without being subjected to the stress of tomorrow evening, too? At his present rate of progress, he'd have Fern so thoroughly bewitched that she'd probably confide the details of her entire life, should he think to ask for them.

Sharon closed her eyes and stifled a groan. Who would ever have thought, back when she first decided on her course of deception, that the lie would come back to haunt her all these years later? Or that a question as simple as, 'How old are you, Fern?' or, 'When is your birthday?' could pose a threat that would destroy the safe little world she'd created for herself and her child?

'Mommy, look!'

Fern's squeal of delight startled Sharon into awareness of what was happening there and then. Clint stood sideways to the row of targets, his blond head cocked at an angle as he took aim and hit every bull's-eye dead centre, as easily as she might have cracked eggs into a bowl.

She wished she could look away, but was too hypnotised by the strength of his deeply tanned forearms, the play of muscle across his back under the thin cotton of his shirt. It wasn't fair that a man could grow more beautiful over time, while a woman showed her age in a thousand subtle ways. Had he noticed that her breasts weren't quite as high and firm as they'd once been, or that her waist wasn't quite as narrow? Did he remember how she'd looked at nineteen? Did he care?

Without warning, memories crowded in again and swept her back through time with dizzying speed: same place, same season, same people . . .

The sun had set that day unnoticed, outshone by the blaze of attraction between the two of them. At some point Margot had discreetly excused herself, escorted by Clint's friend, both of them fully aware that four made a crowd.

Sharon and Clint had strolled away from the fairground and over the bridge to the deserted side of the river. Above them on the bluff, the town's most exclusive homes, the Dunns' among them, had glimmered with lamplight, but down on the strip of sand it was dim and private.

'What do you want from life?' Clint had asked, looking up at the houses. 'To be rich like them?'

The answers had fallen out of her mouth with easy familiarity. 'No,' she'd said. 'To take the fashion world by storm. To be an international name.'

But under cover of dusk her eyes had looked at him and her heart had said, I want you.

He'd been quiet for a minute or two. When he'd finally spoken, his voice had been even huskier than usual. 'Are you hungry?' he'd asked, folding Sharon's fingers in his.

She'd shaken her head, bewitched, bedazzled. Who needed mortal food?

'Neither am I,' he'd said, and she had known that he was telling only half a truth, that what she heard in his voice went beyond the flirtatious curiosity of youth to full-blown adult desire.

She'd been adept enough at fending off lanky boys with peach fuzz for beards and Adam's apples too large for their throats, but this was no baby-faced adolescent trying to muster up the nerve to kiss her. This was a man, with all a man's appetites, and he wanted her. She had known it instinctively, and the power of that knowledge had shot an arrow of heat from her heart to the pit of her stomach.

He'd smiled at her, his eyes inky pools of twilight. She'd looked into their depths and seen the neat blueprint of her life: the secure, comfortable upbringing by well-to-do, society-conscious parents; attendance at all the best schools, membership at all the right clubs; the coveted apprenticeship with a renowned Italian fashion designer. And all at once, none of it had mattered beside the immediacy and urgency of her desire for him.

He'd stopped in the lee of the bluff, under the glimmering green shadows of a maple tree, and had slid his hand around her neck. Not an unfamiliar experience, she'd have thought; others had done the same before him. But this time was different. He was different. His fingers wove spells over her skin, awaking sensations in other parts of her body—hot, quivering, deliciously frightening sensations that left her mind swirling and clouded her judgement.

When he had finally dropped his mouth to her ear, then down to her neck, it was so unlike anything she'd known before that it might have been the first time she'd ever been kissed. Another hot, damp revelation swept her far away from all the touchstones of familiarity. It had been like falling off the edge of the earth. Every stable facet of her life had spun out of control with the touch of his lips. She'd started shaking like a leaf in a storm, had turned her face to his, blindly seeking a closer contact, and, if it was possible to imprint one's heart on another's mouth, she'd imprinted hers on his.

He had seemed taken aback, had held her away from him, a sudden suspicion banking his fire. 'How old are you, Sharon?' he'd asked, his voice a raspy whisper.

And that was when she'd come face to face with the most dangerous choice she'd had to make in her short and hitherto uncomplicated life. Because she'd known that, desire and attraction notwithstanding, he was a man of conscience. There was an integrity about him that would not allow him to satisfy his own raging needs by taking advantage of someone still half a girl.

Tell him the truth, vanishing sanity had warned her, and you'll be safe. He'll run like the wind and you'll never see him again.

She had opted for the other choice, taken the path that led away from everything circumspect and honourable and familiar. 'Twenty-three,' she'd lied, twining her arms around his neck and pulling his head down so that she could find his mouth again. 'Old enough to know what I'm doing.'

She'd pressed herself against him, the fire raging from her nipples to her knees. When he'd tried to restrain her, muttering about public places and people who might walk by and disturb them, she'd squirmed and undulated, a shockingly wanton hussy bent on having her way.

His resistance hadn't lasted long. She'd gloried in the knowledge of his arousal, and continued to torment him with a recklessness that still made her blush all these years later. She'd let her hands roam shamelessly, and at last pushed him past the point of no return.

'Over here,' he'd urged hoarsely, and had stumbled with her to a pale swath of embankment that jutted out into the river beyond the screen of an overhanging willow tree.

The sand had felt cool and grainy against her skin, but his hands had been warm, his mouth hot and hungry. She hadn't been wearing a bra, just a simple top with shorts and a pair of bikini underpants. He'd pushed them all aside, snapped open his blue denim cut-offs.

She'd lost her nerve then, had wanted to cry out that she'd changed her mind, but it had been too late. The words had choked on a gasp as he entered her. She'd tensed at the stabbing pain, then clung to him in fearful wonder as her body accepted him. He'd groaned, driven by demons of her making, and lost himself inside her.

It had been quick and intense, and when it was over he'd looked down at her and, even though it was almost dark, she'd known that his eyes were flat with disgust—for himself and for her. 'You lied,' he'd said, and rolled over the hard sand, away from her.

Pain, shame and fear finally took their toll, and she'd started to cry.

'Straighten your clothes,' he'd said, unmoved. 'I'm taking you home.'

'What if I get pregnant?' she'd whimpered, when what she'd really wanted to say was, Please fall in love with me, the way I've fallen in love with you.

'God forbid!' he'd replied.

The tears had gushed forth at that, an endless torrent that had alarmed him. 'Hey,' he'd said, hauling her to her feet and brushing the sand from her shoulders. 'Sharon, I'm sorry. It was my fault.'

'I didn't mean to be a virgin,' she'd sobbed, and, after a startled minute of silence, he'd half laughed and put his arms around her.

'We all start out that way,' he'd comforted her. 'It's no big deal.'

'Does that mean I'll see you again?' she'd asked on a breath frail with hope.

Although he still had his arms around her, she'd felt his withdrawal. 'Sure,' he'd said. 'Give me your phone number and I'll call you tomorrow.'

She'd wondered, if her lie had been one tenth as unconvincing as his, why he'd ever chosen to believe her when she'd told him she was twenty-three. Of course he hadn't called, not until three weeks later, and by then the suspicion that there might be consequences to her rash behaviour had begun to crystallise into certainty.

'A girl can't get pregnant the first time,' Margot had assured her naïvely, when Sharon had confided her fears.

But Sharon had grown light-years older than Margot since the day she'd met Clint, and she knew better. Girls who gave themselves easily, irresponsibly to men deserved all the trouble they brought on themselves.

'Mommy! Look what Mr Bodine won for me!'

Fern's squeak of delight echoed down the time tunnel, pulling her back to the uncertain haven of the present. She followed it gladly, relief at being freed from the humiliation of her memories outweighing her apprehension at what tomorrow might hold.

'Two teddy bears?' She hoped her smile wasn't quite as wan as her voice. 'How lovely, sweetheart.'

Clint was watching her far too closely. 'Either you're on the verge of collapse,' he observed, bathing her in a smile that had her heart flopping around like an injured bird, 'or you've just seen a ghost. Which is it, dear heart?'

'The ghost,' she admitted. The only trouble was that ghosts were ephemeral, figments of an overwrought imagination, and Clint Bodine was real, never more handsome or desirable, and never more forbidden.

CHAPTER FOUR

THE rehearsal dinner was held in the Tudor room of the Gables Hotel, the town's second-best establishment after the Crescent Creek country club, where the wedding reception was to take place. Fern didn't attend the dinner after all. She'd been out of sorts earlier, and a good night's rest seemed in order if she was to be at her best for the big day itself.

'But you go out and enjoy yourself, Mrs McClure,' Bertha, the housekeeper, insisted. 'I'll be glad to keep an eye on her. She's overtired, that's all. Too much rich food and excitement, if you ask me.'

That, or divine intervention! Clint wouldn't have the chance to worm incriminating information out of her daughter tonight, at least, and it occurred to Sharon that if she had any brains at all she'd steer clear of him, too. But the idea of spending the evening in Clint Bodine's company attracted her much as a flame drew a moth.

'What if she wakes up and needs me?' she murmured, leaning over Fern and making a last pitiful stab at being sensible.

'I'll phone the hotel,' Bertha said, shooing her towards the door. 'Go out and have some fun. Heaven knows you've earned a night off.'

Back in her own room, Sharon took stock of the clothes she'd brought with her. What had seemed more than adequate a week ago struck her now as woefully uninspired. The aquamarine shantung sheath embroidered with seed pearls was reserved for the wedding itself. The fuchsia *palazzo* pants and matching top were strictly for evenings at the house.

The dress she had originally selected for the rehearsal dinner—a polished cotton rose-covered print with a crinoline skirt and portrait collar—no longer struck the right note. It was too blatantly romantic, too reminiscent of the naïve girl who'd flung herself at Clint Bodine ten years ago.

That left the all-purpose basic black. Pencil-slim skirt that just skimmed her knees, short sleeves, plain scoop neck. Black silk stockings, the old-fashioned kind held up with a scrap of lace that passed for a garter belt, and black peau-de-soie pumps with three-inch heels.

A very tasteful ensemble, no doubt, except that it left her looking like a Russian tragic heroine about to fling herself under the wheels of an on-rushing train, all pale-faced, hollow-cheeked and colourless— except for her eyes, which glowed like agitated fireflies. Something else was needed.

Searching through her accessories, she found a length of black chiffon, shot through with gold thread and spangled with coin-sized gold polka dots. Flung around her shoulders, it relieved her aura of impending doom. Plain gold jewellery, every last ounce eighteen-carat, hanging cool at her throat and ears added a touch of classic elegance which gave her confidence a badly needed boost. A splash of Paloma Picasso, a touch of coral lip gloss, a sweep of mascara, a feathering of blusher, and that was the best she could do, given her limited options. But if she didn't look like a million dollars, at least she no longer resembled someone draped in mourning.

The Tudor Room overlooked the river, and as it was such a fine, warm night tables had been set out on the tiled patio. At least thirty guests were already assembled, and Clint didn't see Sharon arrive. Not that he would have noticed had there been only a handful of people present. He was too busy charming Margot's maternal grandmother, a lady who, at seventy-something, was old enough to know better than to respond to such overtures by flapping her eyelashes and cooing like a teenager.

To her credit, the mother of the bride showed more discernment, and continued to treat Clint with undimmed disapproval. He might look disgracefully handsome and distinguished in his pale grey suit, but it took more than a European tailor and a few yards of fine fabric to sway a woman like Vera Dunn. He was an interloper at her daughter's wedding, not someone of *her* choosing, and she was not about to forgive him readily for being so crass.

It was an example she would do well to follow, Sharon had to remind herself more than once as dinner progressed and Clint, beyond a brief greeting, paid her no attention whatsoever. She might have excused him for that, since the seating plan had her placed at a table reserved for out-of-town relatives of the groom and other nondescript hangers-on, while Clint, as one of the ushers, was obliged to sit at the head table. But what she couldn't forgive was his blatant enjoyment at finding himself flanked by bridesmaids disposed to hang on his words as if they had issued from the lips of the Almighty Himself.

Calling on her extensive repertoire of social graces to get her through the ordeal of the evening, Sharon tried to ignore him. It wasn't easy. Despite her best efforts, she found her glance turning repeatedly to where he lounged with negligent grace between two pretty bridesmaids, found her ear attuned to the deep, lazy currents of his laughter. And, worst of all, found herself almost gagging on the bitter dregs of jealousy at his attention not once straying to where she sat.

Dessert was served buffet-style. It was by accident with, perhaps, a little help from design that Sharon managed to wedge herself between Clint and one of his dinner companions, Margot's cousin Genevieve, who appeared too totally under his spell to notice she was in imminent danger of falling out of her low-necked dress.

'Please excuse me,' Sharon murmured, interspersing herself between Clint and the cleavage. 'I'd like to help myself to the fruit *compôte*.'

Clint managed to tear his gaze away from Genevieve long enough to spare Sharon a smile that amounted to little more than a grimace of his finely modelled lips. 'Perhaps I'll do the same,' he said. 'The raspberries are at their best just now.'

'I'd have thought cheesecake was more to your taste,' Sharon couldn't help muttering, with saccharin-coated venom. She was ashamed of herself, she truly was. Genevieve was a nice young woman; that she happened to be generously endowed was no reason to make her the scapegoat of an ex-wife's misplaced envy.

Clint was obviously of the same opinion. His hand closed over Sharon's wrist as she was about to spoon fruit into a stemmed dessert dish. 'Jealous, dear heart?' he enquired softly, his dark blue gaze settling on her with a certain sardonic amusement.

'Hardly!' she scoffed. 'Feast your eyes till they fall out of your head if it affords you pleasure, but don't exhaust yourself too soon. There must be at least five other women still waiting their turn to be ogled.'

'Well, as long as you're not one of them, what do you care?'

'I don't,' she said, and wished it were true. Yet the sad fact was, his words stung her to the quick.

'But?' His fingers continued to restrain her with easy, inflexible strength.

'There are no "buts",' she said, trying to shake him loose.

'Liar,' he mocked. 'You've looked as though you had a sour pickle lodged in your throat from the moment you got here tonight, and, since I'm probably the cause, why don't you spit it out and have done with—if you'll forgive the figure of speech?'

She'd cast sound judgement to the winds and forgive him almost anything—except showing a preference for the company of other women. She must be running a fever!

'I'm worried about Fern,' she improvised. 'You made such a monumental fuss over her yesterday that a person might have been forgiven for thinking you actually cared about her, but it seems to have escaped your notice that she's not here tonight.'

'Oh, I'd noticed,' he said calmly, 'but you *are* here, so there can't be much wrong with her.'

He was too clever for her by half, with a rebuttal ready almost before she'd had time to think up a response to his first charge. 'There isn't,' she admitted. 'She's overtired, that's all, and so am I.' Catching him off guard, she twisted her wrist free and turned away from the buffet. 'And I've changed my mind. I don't want dessert, after all.'

'You've had enough of this shindig?'

'More than enough.'

Ignoring Mrs Dunn's glare of disapproval, he plopped his own portion of raspberries back into the serving bowl. 'So have I. Let's get out of here.'

'*Together*?' Sharon felt her jaw drop, and snapped it closed again in a hurry.

Clint sighed, as though she was testing his reserve of patience to the limit. 'Yes, *together*. *Alone* together! Or does that offend your sensibilities past bearing too?'

The unpalatable truth was that she'd been pining for his undivided attention all evening. Now that it was offered, however, pride prevented her from accepting it graciously. 'Well, heaven forbid I should be responsible for depriving your besotted fans of your nauseating attentions.'

Annoyance deepened his irises to near-midnight-blue. 'That was a cheap shot, dear heart. I was merely making pleasant conversation with my dinner partners, not stroking their knees under the table.'

This *was* the same man who, when she'd told him she'd miscarried their baby, had suggested that perhaps there'd never been any baby to begin with and that the entire history of her pregnancy had been just another lie to try to tie him to her. He hadn't always been as unflappably reasonable as he now appeared.

'I wasn't suggesting you were,' she said, choking back a hurt whose scars weren't nearly as well-healed as she'd believed.

'What are you doing, then? Trying to convince me that you've turned into a mean-mouthed, first-class bitch?'

'That's absurd!'

'I don't think so. For reasons I can't fathom, you seem determined to make me dislike you. Well, your strategy isn't working, so cut it out.'

'Don't give me orders. I'm not a child.'

'Then stop behaving like one.' His observant, unblinking stare made her regret having wished he'd make her the sole focus of his attention. 'You're a decent, kind woman under all that hostility, Sharon, and there's nothing wrong with letting it show. So stop being tiresome and let's get the hell out of here.'

He took her hand, slid it beneath his elbow, and secured it firmly by pressing her arm close to his side. 'And please,' he went on, 'stop staring at me as if you think I've got a lethal weapon hidden up my sleeve!'

'Give me back my hand,' she squeaked, tremors racing over her at the contact of his body against hers.

'Shut up,' he said, piloting her across the patio and over the lawn towards a gravelled path that ran beside the river.

She did, because it took all her concentration to keep her wits about her. The muscled discipline of his arm holding her fast evoked memories too potent to ignore, and it was all she could do to hide the fact that, left to its own devices, her body would wilt against his in a heap of willing, pliant flesh.

Clint appeared not to notice. The sun had gone down, and across the water the sounds from the fairground echoed faintly on the still air. 'Now what could be nicer than this?' he asked, looking around at the banks of flowering shrubs that soon shielded them from the hotel.

She struggled to come up with some acidic response, something that would at least restore a smidgen of prudence in her, even if it did reinforce his impression that she'd become poisoned with bitterness, but the fight was seeping out of her. Intellect could debate the wisdom of her actions till the earth stopped turning, but what was the use when her body felt so absolutely right snuggled up against his like that, and her heart felt whole for the first time in almost a decade?

'I can't think of a thing,' she replied, accepting what she'd suspected for the last several days: that being ten years older hadn't left her one whit wiser.

'We had too few moments like this,' Clint remarked quietly.

His ability to tune in to her thoughts in a way he'd never managed to do when they were husband and wife further weakened her in susceptibility. Her body relaxed, moulding itself ever more closely to the warm, firm strength of his. 'I know,' she said.

'I sometimes feel,' he went on, with an intensity that hinted at all manner of lonely regrets, 'that I'll spend the rest of my life trying to forget that we lost a child. If I could change just one thing, it would be for you to have carried that baby to term. I've often wondered, if you had, whether things might not then have turned out differently for us.'

They were softly spoken, kindly intended words, but they accomplished what her own impaired common sense had failed to do. The menace that had dogged her ever since she'd heard he was in town rose up like a spectre to fill her with new dread.

He sensed it at once. 'Don't pull away from me,' he begged, in a low, soothing voice. 'I understand that you can't feel the same way. You have Fern, and for you to wish that we'd found a happier ending together must be a bit like un-wishing those years that brought her into your life.'

But he didn't understand at all, Sharon thought despairingly. He didn't understand that every time he showed her kindness or tenderness he mired her deeper in a guilt she'd never expected to feel.

At the time of their separation, she'd been certain her actions had been justified. She'd seen herself as abandoned by a man too insensitive to comprehend the loss she'd suffered. Two months later, when she'd learned the incredible truth—that she'd conceived fraternal twins, lost only one of them, and showed every indication of carrying the second successfully—she had not for a moment thought of trying to find Clint and convey the news to him, too. She had gone ahead with the divorce, determined not to give him the chance to accuse her of entrapment a second time.

That perhaps she'd inflicted her share of wrong on him, or that she hadn't always understood him either, had never once occurred to her. She'd been so consumed by her own unhappiness that she'd had no energy to spare to think about how he might be coping. In fact he'd made it so plain that he was miserable in their marriage that she'd assumed he'd find nothing but relief in having it over and done with. The hindsight of now discovering that she'd misjudged him did nothing but give rise to a lot of useless regrets. She couldn't change history.

'It's too late for any of that,' she said, as much to herself as to him. 'And you're surely not saying you regret regaining the freedom to pursue those ambitions you had to put on hold when we married?'

He considered the question for so long that at first she thought he'd decided not to answer. 'I suppose I'm glad I had the chance to reconcile dreams with reality,' he finally acknowledged, 'but I don't know that I'll ever accept what it cost me.'

'You wanted to save the world from itself,' she reminisced, smiling a little at the memory of him as he'd been then, so full of heroic deeds waiting to be done, and so full of hope and optimism for what he could achieve that the world couldn't help but be a better place for his having touched it. 'You wanted to right all the wrongs, end all the oppression, fight for the underdog, defeat——'

'Spare me the clichés,' he cut in bitterly. 'I was an idealist who thought a twentieth-century Robin Hood was all it would take to change the course of history. I learned differently, and I find talking about it an infinite bore, so let's change the subject. What about you? Was success as grand and satisfying as you thought it would be?'

'Yes,' she said, because there was no way she could tell him that, if she hadn't found out about Fern, no amount of recognition or success would have made up for losing him. 'Yes, it was quite wonderful. I've been very lucky and very happy.'

He steered her over a footbridge that took them across the river and into the park. 'No regrets, then?'

None. Her lips formed the word. Every self protective instinct she possessed cried out for her to say it. He was looking down at the path in front of them, not at her, and it should have been easy to utter such a small white lie when she'd deceived him with far graver untruths. But she made the mistake of looking at his profile, at his dark, thick lashes, his strong jaw, at his mouth, which could turn so quickly from proud to passionate, from laughter to sorrow. And she found herself tongue-tied, unable to free either herself or him.

He knew it immediately. His hand settled in the small of her back, inching her closer despite her objection. 'Sharon?'

'No!' she whispered, still denying the truth. She'd married Jason—a good man, a kind man—had shelved dreams for reality, and exchanged romance for security. She had matured, accepted the cards that Fate had dealt her, and tried to make the best of them. It wasn't fair for adolescent longing to flare up again. Not fair and not wise.

'Don't be afraid of me,' Clint begged. 'I'm not the same man who hurt you before.'

That much was too clearly true. The years had left him twice as appealing, while events in between had wrought chasms neither of them could ever hope to cross. The magic might have intensified, but how could she condone falling in love with him all over again, after she'd robbed him of the right to know his own child?

'You don't understand,' she protested, with an appalling lack of conviction. 'I meant, "no, no regrets".'

They had reached the fairground. The crowds had thinned out, and some of the booths had already closed down.

'I don't believe you,' Clint said, slowing to a stop at the Ferris wheel, which was unloading the last of its passengers for the night.

The operator shook his head, ready to tell them they'd left it too late for a ride, but, turning his back to Sharon, Clint entered into brief conference with him.

Stuffing something into the back pocket of his boiler suit, the operator broke into a sly grin. 'Go ahead, Mister. It's all yours.'

Before she had time to realise what was happening, Sharon found herself led into the waiting carriage. 'I'm not riding on this thing!' she decided somewhat after the fact, as the operator snapped the safety bar into place.

'Oh, yes, you are,' Clint said, settling beside her and resting his arm along the back of the seat. 'I just bought two tickets.'

And with a creak they were off, swinging backwards and up through the dark, with nothing to anchor them to earth but the strains of the theme from *Moulin Rouge* wafting after them.

'Why are you doing this?' Sharon demanded, squirming as far away from Clint as possible in the confined space.

'Because I want you some place where you can't escape me,' he said, slithering after her. 'You've been running away from me ever since I got back to town, and it's time you stopped and told me why you're so afraid to be alone with me.'

'I was alone with you down there,' she protested, turning her head away and peering over the side of the carriage, because she thought anything was preferable to looking him in the eye.

She was wrong again. They were at the very top of the wheel, and the ground below appeared dizzyingly far away. She closed her eyes hurriedly, and prayed for fortitude and an early release from her present predicament.

Clint's hand closed over her shoulder with the weighty authority of a prison guard. 'Not really, Sharon. You were poised for flight the entire time, and if you could find a way out of here now you'd take it in a flash. However, since you are, in effect, my prisoner, I think you must reconcile yourself to providing me with a few answers.'

'I don't have to reconcile myself to anything,' she assured him tartly, opening her eyes and making a feeble attempt to resuscitate her will-power. 'This ride won't last forever.'

'No?' He raised his eyebrows. 'Perhaps you haven't noticed yet, but we aren't going anywhere.'

He was right. They were still poised at the top of the Ferris wheel. 'We've stopped,' she exclaimed, stating the absurdly obvious, and ventured another timid peek over the edge of the carriage. There was no one waiting to get on, and no one left to get off. The operator had retired to his little booth and was sitting with his feet propped up, a cigarette dangling from his mouth. She and Clint were completely alone, completely cut off from the rest of the world. 'Clint, we're the only people left on this thing, and it's not moving.'

He smiled at her gently. 'I know, dear heart. I bribed the man down there. Now stop stalling and let's get down to business.'

She felt her heart gain speed as apprehension took hold. 'What sort of business are you referring to?'

'When you heard I was back in town, why was your first instinct to run?'

'I didn't want...' She swallowed, searching for an acceptable half-truth. 'Didn't want the past dredged up again. It's too painful.'

'That's too bad,' he replied. 'I came back because I wanted to lay my ghosts to rest. It's been ten years, Sharon, and I'm tired of the same old nightmares. I'm thirty-seven, and wise enough to know you can't run away from yourself or your past. You can only come to terms with them.'

He sifted gentle fingers through her hair. 'You've grown into a fine and lovely woman, but you've also become my albatross, dear heart. I hoped, after a few months and a few women, that you'd have the good grace to fade a little from my mind, but you didn't. No matter where I went, nor how dangerous a mission I undertook, you stayed with me. A few times I found myself deliberately courting death because, somewhere between finding you and losing you, life lost its flavour. But I guess there's some truth to that old saying that only the good die young, because I survived regardless, and no amount of kamikaze foolishness altered the fact that we'd lost our child.'

She'd thought that letting him do the talking was the lesser of two evils, but it wasn't. It was heart-wrenching, and she couldn't bear the sorrow she saw carved on his mouth. 'Stop it,' she begged, on a frail, trembling breath. 'It doesn't help to rake over old hurts like this.'

'It doesn't help to hang on to them, either,' he said soberly, and brought his hand to rest at the base of her ear. 'I want you to set me free, dear heart.'

'How?'

'Tell me you're happy and that you've forgiven me, but make me believe it this time, because I can't carry this load of guilty baggage any longer.'

She, forgive him? 'Clint,' she begged, losing the battle with the tears that streamed down her face and turned all the lights of the fairground into one dazzling jewel of colour.

'Tell me, Sharon.'

She opened her mouth, willing to say anything to put an end to his pain, but all that came out was a sobbing wail. She tried to cover her face, but he imprisoned both her hands in his and held them patiently.

'Take a deep breath, then tell me,' he insisted.

She struggled for control. 'There's nothing to forgive,' she finally managed, brokenly. 'Please stop blaming yourself. Please forget about me. Be happy and go on with your life.'

'I can't do that, Sharon, unless you can convince me that you have no regrets about us and that what we once shared is a closed chapter in your life.'

She'd lied to him so many times before, either out of selfishness or fear; why was it so difficult to lie to him now out of kindness? 'I had forgotten you existed until you showed up here,' she whispered, closing her eyes, because he'd have seen the denial in them otherwise. 'You belong to another era and have no part in my present life at all.'

He let go of her hand, carefully cupped her jaw, and turned her face to his. 'Look at me,' he said.

She did. His eyes were very intent, his mouth very tender. 'I'd have to be brain-dead to believe you really mean that,' he murmured, inching his mouth to hers, hesitantly, experimentally almost.

Then, before either of them could react with the proper response, instinct leapt in and took control.

'Sharon...?' he muttered urgently.

'Clint...?' she breathed, as though to confirm a long-withheld dream.

He kissed her then, a wild, swirling kiss, full of rage for time lost, full of promise for time yet to come, full of hunger for the here and now. And the long, lonely years melted away.

It would always be that way between them. Always.

CHAPTER FIVE

MARGOT'S wedding-day promised buttery heat and silk-blue skies, probably because Mrs Dunn's threatened hysteria, should it have dared to rain, intimidated even the weather into co-operating.

The house hummed with activity all morning long as final preparations swung into high gear. If the phone wasn't ringing constantly, the doorbell was. Flowers, telegrams and last-minute gifts were delivered. In between occurred the sorts of minor crises without which no wedding worth its salt could possibly take place.

Mrs Dunn had no qualms about roping in Sharon to act as general dogsbody about the place, and Sharon was happy to oblige. Anything was better than having time to dwell on what had transpired between herself and Clint the night before.

She had no idea how long they'd remained marooned at the top of the Ferris wheel. How one kiss could drift so effortlessly into another, become charged with raging hunger, and deepen to shocking levels of intimacy in less time than it had taken her to sign her divorce papers, left her more than mystified.

If her brain's response to Clint's overture had been one of numbed astonishment, her body had undergone no such inhibition. Suffocating heat had raced through her. Her heart had turned into one vast echo chamber, its laboured beat thundering in her ears. A fine tremor had possessed her, leaving her quivering like a wind-tossed leaf in autumn.

His lips had been firm, warm, compelling. His tongue had been a devil, tempting her to sample forbidden pleasures. Even though he had insisted on nothing in return, her mouth had succumbed to the covert persuasion in his, offering whatever he chose to take.

He had chosen to take liberties. He had touched her, and she'd done nothing to stop him. His palms had slid down her jaw to her throat, embarking on a tactile exploration that, for all its skilled delicacy, invoked such a flood of arousal in her that she had felt near to choking. His fingertips had traced the scooped neckline of her dress, skimmed audaciously to her breasts. Her nipples had responded by blossoming with an eagerness that, in blushing retrospect, was downright wanton. And all the time his mouth had woven its wicked spells, seducing hers without mercy.

'Clint...!' Her protest had emerged as insubstantial as thistledown. She had swatted ineffectually at his hands.

'Hush,' he'd commanded against her mouth, and, instead of restraining him, she'd found her own hands changing course and settling on his chest with the tremulous joy of a lost traveller finding her way home.

She had relished the heat of his body under the cool silk lining of his jacket, had drowned in the scent that was his alone, a mixture of soap and starch and sandalwood. She had loosened his tie, undone his shirt buttons, run her fingers down the lean symmetry of his ribs, and revelled in the uneven acceleration of his heart.

He had repaid her in kind, falling victim to the same onslaught of passion that seared her. If the tiny voice of caution had attempted to speak to either of them, it had been swept rudely aside, completely vanquished by the raging hunger that possessed them.

That the whole encounter had occurred in a space too precarious and narrow to allow for much activity was entirely due to providence. Given more conducive surroundings, she'd probably have let him strip her naked and kiss every bare inch. She had shown, she decided in the cool disdain of hindsight, about as much moral fibre as a piece of cooked spaghetti.

Clint had come to his senses first, stymied more by her tight-fitting skirt than any other consideration, if his impressively articulate cursing had been anything to go by. But not before his wicked hand had forged a path up past her hem and found the strip of soft flesh where her silk stockings came to an end. She could never have looked him in the face again had he gone on to discover how embarrassingly damp and aroused she had become by the whole skirmish.

'You're pinning the corsage to my skin, Sharon!'

Mrs Dunn's pained shriek rescued her from memories too discomfiting to be borne. How could she have allowed an ex-husband such liberties? How could she have reciprocated with such unbridled enthusiasm?

'Sorry,' she mumbled, and managed to stab herself with the pin instead. 'Ouch!'

'Don't get blood on my gown, you inept fool!'

It was a description she deserved, albeit for reasons Mrs Dunn mercifully could never conceive. Given her prior record, she had to be an incredible fool to have believed that she could spend time in the company of Clint Bodine and retain control of her emotions. He had beguiled her once in the space of a few hours, and come close to doing so again.

'Stop dilly-dallying and get on with it, Sharon,' Mrs Dunn complained. 'The wedding's today, not next week. The limousines are waiting, and so is everyone else.'

Including Clint, Sharon thought in resignation.

Though fragrant with roses and jasmine, the church was dimly cool, unlike the day outside. Henrietta Barr, the organist, played Beethoven's 'Ode to Joy' without a single mistake, and followed it with an equally flawless rendition of Pachelbel's Canon in D, no doubt aware that a less than perfect performance would incur the full magnitude of Mrs Dunn's wrath.

Sharon, seated in the second pew on the left, fiddled with the diamond-studded bracelet on her wrist and prayed for the fortitude to survive the rest of the day without further compounding her errors or compromising her integrity. If God would grant her that much, she'd take responsibility for the rest of her life herself, starting tomorrow.

The next flight out of Crescent Creek left at noon tomorrow. Barring a major catastrophe on a par with the eruption of Krakatoa, she and Fern would be on that flight and Clint would again be consigned to the past, where he best belonged. However, if, between now and then, he was crass enough to gloat over what had transpired on that benighted Ferris wheel, she'd shove him and his rented suit head-first in the river.

Not that she really had cause to worry, she conceded wryly, as the grandmother of the bride paraded down the aisle on the arm of the chief usher, to the strains of a prelude by Bach. Apparently as anxious as she to forget the whole shabby incident, Clint was one of the few who hadn't phoned or dropped by the house that morning. She'd heard not a word from him since he'd left her at the Dunns' front door.

He'd been almost as uncommunicative when he'd brought her home, escorting her through the park and up the long driveway to the house in the sort of dazed silence that suggested he was at a complete loss to understand why he'd just succumbed to the same sort of crazy impulse that had landed him in a mess of married misery once before.

Once arrived on the doorstep, he'd taken her key from her hand and inserted it in the lock. It was the time when, given a normal man and woman in a normal situation, she might have asked him in for a night-cap. At the very least, she might have offered her cheek for a kiss. She'd done neither, fumbling her way instead through half a dozen attempts to voice a coolly poised dismissal that had emerged as a string of, 'I don't think—er... It would be best if—er... What I mean is...'

Pathetic!

At first he'd waited for her to wind down with the same weary patience he'd shown after their first sexual encounter ten years earlier. It was the most enduring emotion she seemed able to inspire in him once he'd had his way with her, she reflected gloomily.

Finally he'd cut short her babblings by articulating a strangled, 'Goodnight,' then beating such a hasty retreat that, if she'd pinned any hopes of a reconciliation on their furtive little scuffle above the fairground, they'd have died a fast death on the spot.

Since such an occurrence was not in any way a viable option, she was very glad. Just as she was very glad that when she had arrived at the church door a few minutes ago it had fallen to one of the other ushers to escort her to her seat. Clint had been occupied elsewhere—probably commiserating with the groom—for which she was truly grateful, because she didn't think she could have tolerated walking down the aisle on his arm. That particular stroke of irony would have shattered what frail composure she'd managed to recruit.

'Darling girl!' a familiar voice exclaimed in hushed tones, and Miss Celeste Bodine eased her chubby hips on to the pew beside Sharon. 'You look so lovely. Doesn't she look lovely, Jubilee?'

'A picture. She'll outshine the bride in that dress,' Miss Jubilee boomed, in such carrying tones that Sharon shrank in her seat. 'Don't you think so, Clinton?'

And there he was after all, leaning over his aunts with that charming blend of flirtatious solicitude that unfailingly endeared him to them, and so disgustingly handsome in his white jacket and black tie that Sharon feared she'd melt on the spot.

He looked her over, an evil glint in his larkspur-blue eyes. 'Quite possibly,' he agreed blandly, 'though whoever it was that claimed clothes make the woman missed the mark as far as I'm concerned. It's what lies underneath the outward trappings that really counts.'

Sharon flicked her gaze toward the altar, away from his face and that infuriating knowing smile. Oh, he'd wind up in the river yet!

Clint grinned, slid into the pew behind her, and leaned close enough that the perfume from the fresh violets pinned to the brim of her hat left him almost light-headed. She stared straight ahead, doing an excellent job of projecting just the right degree of aloof displeasure. A less foolhardy man would have run for cover. He didn't budge.

'I know just what you're thinking,' he whispered in her ear. 'You find me an insufferable boor and would consider it a stroke of the utmost good fortune if I'd quietly slink back under my rock and stop embarrassing you in public.'

'Not just in public,' she muttered through clenched teeth. 'I find you obnoxious at all times.'

'Really?' He exhaled gently against her neck, and felt enormous pleasure when she shivered as though caught in the teeth of a winter gale. 'You have a funny way of showing it.'

'Unless there's a point you're trying to make with all this drivel, shouldn't you be attending to more pressing things, such as ushering guests to their proper places?' she enquired, sitting up a little straighter, squaring her shoulders more firmly, and jutting out her chin in a manner that suggested—in the politest possible terms, of course—that she'd like to roast him on a spit over red-hot coals.

She might have fooled most people, but he wasn't 'most people', and the sooner she accepted that, the better. He saw beyond that perfectly controlled, perfectly lovely facade, and he wasn't deceived for a minute. 'You can spend the rest of the day with your eyes fixed on the flower arrangements as though you expect dancing aphids to spring out at any minute, Sharon,' he said softly, 'but that won't deter me in the slightest.'

'I haven't the faintest idea what you're talking about.'

He lifted a skein of her hair and held it up to the multi-coloured light spilling through the stained-glass windows. It glimmered faintly blue-black, and slid between his spread fingers with the same fluid grace as its owner. She tried to yank herself free, but stopped short when she realised he still held her captive by a strand.

Disregarding Aunt Jubilee's less than subdued snort of glee, he leaned further under the wide brim of Sharon's hat and planted a soft kiss at the base of her ear. 'Do you really think that if you ignore me I'll be persuaded to forget what took place between us at the top of that Ferris wheel?'

'I had hoped you might,' she muttered stiffly.

He let go of her hair. 'Then you sadly underestimate me, dear heart,' he replied. 'What started out less than a week ago as a simple mission to unload my guilt and win your absolution has taken one unexpected turn too many.'

He stood up, did a smart about-turn, and marched back down the aisle, his grin fading into a gravity that more accurately reflected his true state of mind.

In the beginning he had hoped the surprise of his reappearance in her life would take her off guard and hand him an easy victory. What he had not foreseen was his own response to seeing her again, which was turbulent in a way he could neither have explained nor anticipated. So many women grew coarse and unkempt as they grew older—'let themselves go', as the aunts were fond of saying. But Sharon had grown lovelier, and no amount of self-scorn could repress his constant urge to look at her for the complicated pleasure it afforded him. He saw a remote dark-haired, green-eyed stranger who'd once been his wife and once—with tragic brevity—carried his child. He couldn't believe how painful he found that knowledge. Enter problem number one.

Her reaction to seeing him again in some ways struck an odder note still. She appeared weighed down by an even greater guilt than his. On top of that, she was desperate to hide the fact that she was clearly afraid of him. He remembered too well that peculiar brand of wily naïveté that had been her trademark at nineteen not to recognise it in more subtle form today. She was up to something, and it had to do with him. Enter problem number two.

However, since he was not a man to be easily discouraged, he'd laid a trap to outmanoeuvre her. He'd freely admit he had devious intent in mind when he'd arranged for the two of them to be marooned on top of the Ferris wheel. He'd been prepared to spend all night there if that was what it took to get the answers he was looking for.

He'd even gone so far as to decide that the shock effect of a kiss might surprise her into spilling out the secrets she seemed so determined to keep from him. And he'd been damn sure it was all that was needed to settle the ambivalent feelings that plagued him.

But things had gone awry with dismaying speed. A kiss hadn't been enough. A touch hadn't been enough. And when that icy control of hers had crumbled in the heat of a fervour she couldn't disguise, his game plan had backfired with startling consequences. What followed had played havoc with his emotions and hell with his hormones. Ten-year-old feelings had revived, fresh as yesterday. He hadn't been prepared for that, or the fear that suddenly had hold of him.

He didn't understand it. Here he was, a man who'd learned to live by his wits and reflexes—someone who could land an aeroplane on a field the size of a postage stamp, fulfil a mission, take off with enemy artillery blasting around him, and still keep a cool head. Yet the truth was this little bit of a woman scared him witless. He couldn't shake the suspicion that she held his future in the palm of her hand and could destroy him as easily as most people could swat a mosquito.

Enter problem number three, because, no matter how badly he wanted to, he couldn't shrug off the feelings, and he wasn't going to take them home with him when this week was over. He hadn't gone to all the trouble of tracking her down just to exchange one load of hang-ups for another.

She could wallow all she liked in outrage and chagrin, but he wasn't going to be a good sport and disappear until he'd come up with answers to all his questions. And if she thought playing the Ice Maiden might discourage him, she should have given it a try *before* last night, because the performance came too damned late to be convincing. He was more determined than ever to get to the bottom of the mystery concerning his beautiful ex-wife.

'The bride's arrived,' one of his fellow ushers informed him. 'The minister wants us to go around to the side-door of the vestry, where Alan's waiting to be led to the slaughter.'

'Good. It's time this show got rolling,' Clint said.

Henrietta Barr paused in her recital, and an expectant hush fell over the congregation. The minister took up his position; the groom strode bravely out of the waiting area, accompanied by his attendants. Sharon took a deep breath and turned her eyes firmly away from Clint. She would not dignify his ambiguous little threats by sparing them another thought.

The opening chords of the 'Trumpet Voluntary' boomed forth, and the congregation turned to watch the bridal procession. Fern came first, delicious in flower-sprigged silk organza, and so starry-eyed with wonder and excitement that Sharon vowed anew that she'd move heaven and earth before she'd let anything hurt her daughter. And it would hurt her, dreadfully, to discover that Jason wasn't really her father.

Unbidden, Sharon's eyes swivelled to Clint in time to catch him drop a slow outrageous wink at Fern, who promptly burst into nervous giggles. The rest of the bridesmaids took up their places and waited for Margot, who drifted down the aisle on her father's arm, looking ethereal in a cloud of silk and lace.

The organ notes faded away as the minister began in one of those rich, solemn voices that lent dramatic impact to the most ordinary proclamations. Fern stared at him, mesmerised, seemingly convinced that he was possessed of supernatural powers. Margot and

Alan locked gazes, oblivious to anyone but each other. Mrs Dunn started to cry in the restrained, well-bred sort of fashion acceptable on such occasions. Miss Celeste smiled, and Miss Jubilee blew her nose with the vigour of a trumpeter swan.

Clint chose to stare at Sharon unblinkingly. He had no manners at all, she decided, and tried to look away, but the familiar words of the traditional marriage ceremony reached out to haunt her.

'An honourable estate, not to be enterprised unadvisedly, lightly, but reverently, discreetly...'

'... If you're pregnant, I suppose we'd better not waste any time getting married...'

'Don't feel obligated. I'm a modern, independent woman, and I promise my father won't come after you with a shotgun,' she'd said, knowing full well that she was terrified both at how her parents might react and at what the future held. What she most needed at that moment was to have Clint tell her he loved her and that he was happy and proud to acknowledge her as his wife.

Unlike her, though, he felt under no compunction to mince words. 'There were other things I had in mind, I admit, but...'

'Into which holy estate these persons present come now to be joined...'

She'd never forget her own wedding day. Not joyful with summer sunshine, like this one of Margot's, nor even angry with storms, but prophetically grey and overcast. Sullen. A man and a woman taking part in a ceremony not blatantly happy but prudently furtive, and left trapped in a marriage filled with guilt and resentment.

For the first time she'd fully understood the import of that damning word, 'entrapment'. But she'd been too young and cowardly to set Clint free and had justified the union by saying that she loved him too much to lose him. Now she knew that if she'd really loved him enough she'd have let him go.

From his position near the altar, Clint stared at her unwaveringly. She tried again to tear herself free. Once again, he refused to release her.

Not normally given to paranoid fantasies, Clint couldn't escape the feeling that the words being directed at Alan and Margot were really intended for him.

'Wilt thou have this woman...love her, comfort her, honour, and keep her in sickness and in health...?'

What a pitiful failure he'd been at that, too busy being furious at himself for his irresponsible bachelor's ways two months earlier, instead of focusing on his husbandly obligations now. Sharon had been plagued by morning sickness, and he'd been glad to get away from the house for days at a time, because the sight of her pale little face left him feeling like a brute. So much for looking after her 'in sickness and in health'.

As for comforting her... She'd miscarried in the apartment that he'd rented in a house a few streets removed from his aunts' place. He hadn't been there at the time, of course, and by the time he got back to town he'd found her paler and more fragile than ever. And more unreachable.

'To my wedded wife, to have and to hold from this day forward...'

Much later that night, when he'd thought she was asleep, her voice had come out of the darkness, full of pain and sadness.

'There's no reason for us to stay married now, is there?'

'I suppose not,' he'd said, and assumed that it was his own sense of loss that made the prospect of freedom seem less thrilling than he'd expected.

'What will you do?'

'Pick up where I had to leave off, I guess. What about you?'

'Go on with my apprenticeship,' she'd said. 'It doesn't start until the beginning of the year, so I haven't missed anything.'

She was just a schoolgirl, he'd thought, and he'd hurtled her into womanhood in the most painful way possible. 'Will you be all right? About losing the baby, I mean.'

Her voice had been full of a grief he hadn't wanted to hear. 'It's probably for the best. Neither of us has been happy these last few weeks.'

But it hadn't been for the best, because they'd both been haunted by what they'd lost, not just in terms of their child, but in the snuffing out of a relationship that, given proper time to grow, might have withstood the worst that life had to throw at it.

She was remembering, too. Across the aisle, her eyes shone greener than water, full of tears. Wounded. By him. To his horror, his own vision blurred and he had to look away.

CHAPTER SIX

THE reception was a nightmare. It seemed to take forever before the speeches were over and the dancing finally began. By the time Clint led Fern on to the floor, the strain of seeing him once again thrown into such proximity with his own daughter threatened to unhinge Sharon.

Allowing a barely decent interval to elapse, she made the move to put an end to her misery. 'May I cut in?'

'You want to dance with me?' Clint's raised eyebrows betrayed his astonishment at her request.

Not really, she felt like replying, but I've had enough of standing helplessly by and leaving my daughter at the mercy of your not so harmless questions.

Fern had walked down the aisle on her father's arm after the ceremony, both of them looking absurdly pleased with the arrangement. She and Clint had posed side by side for the photographer, thereby fixing in perpetuity a similarity in their smiles that Sharon had never before noticed but which now seemed glaringly apparent. Fern had sat next to Clint at the endless seven-course dinner. And throughout, the best Sharon had been able to do was try to lip-read from a distance and pray Fern wasn't indicting her mother by exposing a minefield of information to Clint's scrutiny.

So, 'I'd love to dance with you,' she said, 'if you don't mind, honey.'

'Not a bit,' Clint said.

'I wasn't asking you,' Sharon snapped. 'I was asking Fern.'

'Mommy wouldn't call you "honey".' Fern giggled. 'She doesn't know you enough.'

'You're absolutely right, sweet pea,' Clint agreed, the smile he bestowed Sharon's way reminiscent of a hungry barracuda on the prowl. 'Mommy doesn't know me nearly as well as she thinks she does. Shall we dance, Sharon?'

'I won't be long,' Sharon told Fern, and submitted to having Clint loop his arm around her waist as though they were on the best and most familiar of terms.

Fern examined the sight with frank approval. 'Be long,' she recommended. 'I'll be all right. I'll dance by myself and make my dress spin out like this, see?' And she executed a pirouette to demonstrate.

'It might be better if you found a less crowded spot to do that,' Sharon suggested. 'You'll crash into someone otherwise.'

'And end up flat on your bum.' Clint widened his eyes and made a face to great comic effect, sending Fern into paroxysms of mirth.

'Mommy doesn't let me say "bum",' she squeaked, taking immediate advantage of the chance to do just that. 'She says it's not a word ladies use.'

Sharon tried to keep a straight face. 'Especially not in polite society.'

'Then I guess I owe you and Mommy an apology.' But Clint didn't look sorry, and Sharon could feel the laughter shaking him. 'Why don't you practise your pirouettes outside while I dance with her and try to make amends?'

'But stay close to the clubhouse, where I can see you,' Sharon cautioned her.

The minute they were alone, Clint's arm snaked more resolutely around her waist and drew her a good deal closer than Emily Post would have considered proper. It felt divine.

'It was a lovely wedding service, wasn't it?' Sharon asked brightly, hoping to disguise the giddy discombobulation he invoked.

'Take that phoney smile off your face,' he growled back. 'It doesn't suit you or the occasion. And no, it was a lousy wedding service, at least as far as you and I were concerned. So lousy, in fact, that you cried.'

Trust him to have noticed! And what did he mean—'It doesn't suit the occasion'? What had he discovered? 'Women always cry at weddings,' she said guardedly, her smile evaporating.

'But not for the reasons that your eyes were swimming, dear heart,' he replied, sweeping her into a reverse turn, then bending her backwards in a Clark Gable dip that demonstrated a superb mastery of dance techniques, regardless of what he'd once told Fern. 'They weren't tears of happiness. They were brought on by the unhappy memory of our own less than glamorous nuptials.'

She clutched the silk lapel of his jacket with her free hand and stifled a squeak. 'As if I still care!' she gasped, as much in relief that they were on a safe topic as the fact that he'd almost literally swept her off her feet.

He straightened her up again without missing a beat. 'Stop playing cute games, Sharon. You'd have to be some sort of saint not to resent that shabby little ceremony we called a wedding. As I recall, you didn't have even a bouquet, let alone a long white gown or a veil. You wore a pale green dress and your grandmother's pearls. And your parents were very disapproving.'

'You wore grey trousers with a navy blazer,' she said soberly, surprised that he should have remembered. 'And while my parents looked positively stony-faced, your aunts smiled and cried at the same time. Afterwards we went back to their house and they served us a lunch of cold salmon and a wedding-cake that they'd made themselves and decorated with fresh flowers from the garden.'

'But your family didn't join us.'

'No,' she said, long since resigned to the alienation from her parents that had never fully healed. 'They had to rush back to catch a flight to Florida, where my father was playing in a golf tournament.'

Clint's voice was almost tender. 'You didn't have much to make the day special, did you?'

I had you, she wanted to tell him, and you were all I ever wanted. Not even her mother's outrage or her father's disappointment had been enough to make her doubt that. 'There wasn't time for anything more elaborate, and it wouldn't have been appropriate, given the circumstances.'

He held her slightly away from him so that he could search her face. 'What circumstances are those?'

As if he couldn't guess! Once her parents had learned of her condition, all their plans for a society wedding on their home turf had been abandoned. 'I absolutely could not face people,' her mother had exclaimed, wrinkling her aristocratic nose in distaste. 'I suppose we should be grateful that you've retained enough decency to get this charade of a wedding out of the way before you start to show.'

'I was the pregnant bride of an unwilling bridegroom,' Sharon said baldly, meeting Clint's gaze without flinching. 'Hardly what you'd call cause for celebration.'

'Did you feel terribly cheated, Sharon?' he asked, and although his expression remained the same there was a world of sadness in his voice.

'If I did,' she said carefully, touched more than she cared to admit, 'I got over it when I became Jason's wife. At least he wasn't coerced into marrying me.'

'I wasn't exactly dragged to the altar kicking and screaming the whole way, you know.'

'You realise, of course,' her mother had declared with daunting certainty, 'that the only reason that man is doing the right thing by you is the fact that your father would horse-whip him if he refused?'

'You weren't exactly over the moon about it, either,' Sharon said, snuffing out her mother's unpleasant contention. 'And afterwards there was so much unspoken resentment that it was like a wall between us. You were very unhappy with me, Clint.'

'I was unhappy with *me*,' he said. 'I blamed myself for the mess we were in.'

She didn't want to get started on the topic of blame. It opened too many doors she had to keep closed. 'Why don't we just forget it? It all happened a long time ago.'

He manoeuvred them to a corner of the dance-floor that was less crowded. 'Don't try to palm me off with platitudes like that, for Pete's sake! It's bothered me ever since we separated that I didn't see the hazards soon enough to steer us around them. There might have been magic between us, Sharon, if things had started out differently. Instead, we wound up in a union held together by guilt and baling wire. If ever a couple came into marriage for all the wrong reasons, we did. We ended up blaming each other, and looking for excuses to walk away from it all.'

'We both made mistakes,' she said, 'and we can't change them at this late date, any more than we can turn back the clock. Too much has happened since for that to be possible.'

'I didn't go to the trouble of tracking you down with the expectation that we could,' he assured her deflatingly. 'All I hoped was that time and distance would give us the perspective to talk things over without recrimination, that we might somehow absolve each other for our sins of omission and commission and, in the full realisation that there's never any way of going back, at least lay the past to rest and find some peace.'

But the past and the present had become so hopelessly intertwined since he'd walked back into her life that Sharon didn't know if her conscience would ever allow her another day's real peace. 'At the risk of annoying you with yet another platitude,' she said, the hope that he might agree feeble, to say the least, 'sometimes it's better to let sleeping dogs lie.'

'A week ago, I'd have said that was certainly a possibility,' he said, 'but then I saw you again and some very strange things started to happen, Sharon—and please don't insult my intelligence by pretending you don't know what I'm talking about.'

Alarm shot through her because she *didn't* know for sure; that was the whole problem. Had Fern let drop some piece of information that had set in motion a dangerous curiosity on his part? Or was he referring to other kinds of feelings—the sexual sort that flared between a man and a woman, torching the atmosphere with electricity? The sort that Sharon was finding increasingly disturbing and hard to ignore.

She risked a peek at his face and decided that if he had the slightest suspicion that Fern was his daughter his primary response would be one of rage rather than regret. His words would be flaying her alive, not sweeping over her in sensual waves.

'It's just nostalgia,' she said, with false airiness. 'It happens all the time at weddings. You see a couple as happy as Margot and Alan and you can't help making comparisons and wishing the same for your own life. Silly, isn't it, when the feelings just aren't there any more?'

He pulled her closer and wrapped his arm more tightly around her waist. Without releasing hers, he brought his other hand up and with his forefinger raised her chin, then bent his head so that they were dancing almost nose to nose. 'Aren't they?' he asked, his sexy, husky voice sending her heart into a series of pixilated cartwheels. 'Are you sure?'

'What...?'

'I kissed you last night,' he said, dipping his head further under the wide brim of her hat, so that his lips were close enough to graze hers, 'half expecting to get my face slapped for it. But you kissed me back.'

'I did not!' She floundered to bring her coping strategies into play, to appear coolly amused instead of indignantly juvenile. 'My lips were in the way, and you took advantage of them.'

She felt the laughter rumble through his chest. His hand stroked up her spine to the back of her neck. 'This is a lovely bit of nonsense you're wearing,' he countered, dancing her on to the long covered veranda of the clubhouse, 'but it has to go.'

And before she could guess his intent or prevent him, he plucked the straw hat from her head and sent it, Devon violets and all, sailing into the flowerbed in the garden below. 'That's better,' he said complacently. 'Now I can see the lies in your eyes before your mouth gets around to uttering them.'

'What I meant to say,' she amended, stumbling over the words, 'was that you took me by surprise, that's all. If I'd had the slightest inkling of what you had in mind, I *would* have slapped your face.'

'That still doesn't explain why you responded as you did, with a fervour that revived ten-year-old feelings and made them seem fresh as yesterday. I've kissed a lot of women since you and I were a couple, dear heart——'

'Oh, please!' she exclaimed, happy to find herself on solid ground at last. 'Spare me an account of your conquests. I'm really not interested, nor are they any of my business.'

'And not one of them,' he continued, unperturbed by her outburst, 'affected me quite like that little exchange of last night.'

'It's just as well. The sort of liberties you were taking—in a public place, no less—could have landed you in jail.'

'You have that sort of impact on me,' he replied drily. 'I tend to forget all about propriety when I get close to you. Take now, for example. I'm intensely conscious of your lovely body next to me, Sharon. I can feel your breasts, the movement of your hips, the brush of your thighs against mine, and, while I'm somewhat abashed at the results all this proximity is having on me, you ought to be gratified.'

'You're indecent . . . !' she objected, but faintly, because the truth was that propinquity was unleashing devastation on her, too.

'Not to mention despicable,' he agreed, with unruffled good humour, given his previous admission.

'You ought to be ashamed,' she said.

'No, *you* ought to be, because at least I'm honest enough to admit to how I feel, whereas you . . .' He gave her a little shake, but his voice caressed her. 'You, dear heart, pretend you are unmoved when, in fact, you're terrified. The question is, of whom? Me?' He slipped both arms around her waist and drew her snugly against him from chest to knee with potent effect. 'Or of yourself? Which is it, and why, my darling ex-wife?'

Sharon's heart swelled. He made confession sound so easy, and she wished that it were. She ached to be rid of all the deceit, to tell him, 'Fern's your daughter,' but it wasn't the right time. It never *would* be the right time for her and Clint.

He was watching her closely, but she was rescued from having to answer by a high-pitched scream floating up from the gardens. 'Mommy, Mommy!'

Fear washed over Sharon, momentarily paralysing her. 'That's Fern!'

'Good God, what's the matter with her?' Clint gripped her shoulders almost painfully.

Inside the clubhouse the music played on, punctuated by laughter and the clink of crystal on crystal.

'Mommy!' The shriek came again, galvanising both of them to action.

Racing to the waist-high parapet, Sharon leaned over, unmindful of her own safety. 'I'm coming, sweetheart. Where are you?'

Sobbing screams greeted her, electrifying in their distress. Spurred by the knowledge that her child was in terror or pain, and without thought for her own safety, Sharon grabbed at one of the slender stone columns supporting the veranda roof and tried to hurl herself over the parapet, intent only on reaching Fern's side.

She'd made but minor headway before panic seemed to turn her limbs leaden with fear. She lost her impetus and found herself immobilised, with both feet swinging wildly in the air. She could feel nothing but a constriction around her ribs and waist. She could hear nothing but Fern's desperate cries, carried to her in waves as the blood rushed and receded in her ears.

And then, suddenly, sharply, a hand wrenched her head around and Clint's face swam into bleary focus. 'It's a ten-foot drop to the garden, Sharon. Breaking your own neck isn't going to save Fern's,' he said, his voice as firm as his arm hauling her back to the slate floor of the veranda.

'I have to go to her!'

'Of course you do,' he said, 'but not that way.' And, taking her by the hand, he ran with her along the veranda to the steps that led to the grounds below.

Someone else had already found Fern. One of the waiters was crossing the stretch of lawn towards them, carrying her in his arms. An older woman—a guest whom Sharon didn't know—hurried along at his side. By then, Fern's screams had subsided to wheezing sobs.

'She'll be all right, ma'am,' the waiter said to Sharon.

'I came outside to admire the roses, and suddenly heard her scream and saw her struggling on the grass near the flowers over there, so I called for help,' the woman panted. 'I don't know what happened to her.'

Clint studied clusters of angry red lumps on Fern's arms and neck, then rolled back the hem of her dress to inspect her legs. 'I do,' he said, 'and she's not all right at all.'

Fern, her eyes huge and glassy, sought and found Sharon's face. 'Mommy, I hurt,' she whispered on a fractured breath. 'I don't have any air.'

'Should we call an ambulance, do you think?' the woman enquired nervously.

'Yes, please,' Sharon whispered, stroking the hair away from Fern's forehead. Her skin felt clammy and her breathing was frighteningly shallow. 'Fern, darling, what happened?'

'She's been stung by wasps or bees,' Clint said tersely, gesturing for the waiter to hand her over to him, then striding towards the car park on the far side of the clubhouse. 'A whole nest of them, from the looks of it. Forget calling an ambulance; there isn't time.'

Cursing her high, impractical heels, Sharon stumbled to keep pace with him. 'How do you know?'

'I just do,' he said. 'Trust me.'

He was Fern's father, but he didn't know that. He was, to all intents and purposes, a man who'd come back to free himself once and for all from the last vestiges of a marriage that had been a disaster from the first; the same man who'd walked away from her once before when she needed him terribly. There was no reason in the world for her to trust him now, and a week ago she'd have laughed at the very idea. Yet she trusted him anyway. There was no one else she wanted by her side at that moment.

'I do,' she said, 'but Clint, I'm frightened. Why is she breathing like that?'

'Shock.' He shifted Fern to his left arm, and jutted out his right hip. 'My car keys are in here somewhere, Sharon.'

She fumbled in his jacket pocket. 'Yes, I've got them.'

'Open the doors and get in the back seat. Do you know anything about CPR?'

She scrambled inside the car, panic skittering up her spine. 'You mean artificial respiration?'

'Call it whatever you like, as long as you know how to use it.'

'Why?' She heard the shrill edge of hysteria in her voice, fought its gathering momentum.

He loaded Fern on to the back seat and rested her pale little face in Sharon's lap. 'Because this is an emergency. You have to keep a really close eye on her. Check her pulse, her breathing.'

'Her breathing?' Fear surged in Sharon's throat, bitter to the taste. This couldn't be happening! A child—*her child*—did not go from robust good health to deadly danger in the space of a few minutes, not from a bee-sting.

Clint heard the underlying terror. 'Get a grip, Sharon. This is no time to fall apart. Your daughter's life depends on your staying calm.'

'I will.' She struggled for control, drew in a massive, shaking breath. 'I will. Tell me what I should do.'

'Watch her, and be ready to resuscitate her if you have to.'

At that, the panic tore free. 'My God, Clint——!'

'*Watch her*, I said! Keep her airway clear.' Slamming closed the back door, he flung himself into the driver's seat and fired up the engine. 'You can collapse later.'

The car surged forward, spitting gravel from under its tyres and screaming around the curve of the driveway. When they reached the road Clint leaned on the horn and didn't let up until the flashing red light of the Emergency entrance to the Crescent Creek Cottage Hospital reflected off the windscreen.

The noise had alerted the staff. Within seconds Fern was hustled inside on a stretcher. A team of doctors ran beside her, monitoring her vital signs. Clint stayed close, relaying information in concise and logical order.

Sharon crawled out of the car and sagged against the open door. She would have berated herself for the weakness that allowed her to let him take her place at her daughter's side, but she was too busy offering prayers for Fern's recovery to worry about so trivial a point of order.

'Your husband asked me to come and get you. Would you like a wheelchair?' A woman in a pink flowered smock appeared at her side, concern and understanding evident in her soft brown eyes. 'You look a little faint, you know.'

'I'll be fine.' Though it was all Sharon could do to stand upright, the shock was wearing off, displaced by a burning anxiety that focused with sharper cruelty on the reality of what had happened in the course of the last fifteen minutes. 'I just need to be with my daughter, that's all.'

'Yes, of course.' A sympathetic hand slipped around her elbow and guided her inside the building. 'But first you have to give the admissions clerk some information about your little girl. The more we know about her, the better we can help her.'

It took forever. Sharon's patience was in rags long before the last item of personal history had been collated. When she was finally free, Clint was beside her, his expression drawn.

The mere act of voicing the question assaulted her like a physical blow. 'How is she?'

'It's as I thought,' he said, walking her to a couch in an alcove and pressing her into it. 'She disturbed a wasps' nest and got stung about fifteen times.'

Sharon looked at him, searching to find the answer she most needed to hear but was afraid to ask for. Instead she skirted around the subject. 'You talked about resuscitating her, Clint. You didn't want to wait for an ambulance.'

'I know,' he said. 'When I saw that she was having trouble breathing, I realised she could be suffering anaphylactic shock. There——'

'*Anafill-what?*' She'd never before heard the word, couldn't so much as repeat it properly, let alone begin to spell it, but the sound of it struck new terror in her heart. 'What's that?'

'I'm not a doctor, Sharon; I'm just guessing. You're better off to wait and get the facts from someone qualified to explain it all to you.'

But hearing from the experts in no way mitigated the gravity of Fern's condition. Sharon had only to look at Clint to know that. The blue of his eyes looked almost bruised, as though he hated having to share his fears with her.

The inevitable question hammered inside her head, refusing to go unanswered. 'Is she going to die, Clint?'

The minute she'd asked, she'd have done anything to unsay the words. Giving them voice allowed them too much power and did terrible things to her faith.

What would she do without Fern? How would she ever go on?

Everything she felt must have been written on her face, because Clint squatted down on his heels in front of her and held her, sustaining her with his strength and sanity. His warm, husky voice washed over her with more kindness than she had any right to expect from him. 'No, she isn't! I won't let anything happen to your baby, dear heart; you can count on that.'

The irony of his softly spoken words completely undid her. She collapsed against him and burst into tears that she thought would never end.

CHAPTER SEVEN

CLINT had wanted her to lower her guard, but not like this, to the point of utter devastation. The way she felt in his arms—like a crushed flower that someone had trampled carelessly underfoot—filled him with the profound urge to kill anything that threatened her.

'Sweetheart,' he begged, over and over, all the time pressing her face to his shoulder and stroking the crown of her head. 'Sweetheart, it's going to be all right.'

'Please don't let her die,' she sobbed, her voice muffled against his neck.

'I won't,' he promised, and vowed that he'd go toe to toe with God Himself on that pledge if need be. He hadn't been able to prevent her losing her first child, but he'd rearrange the heavens before he'd let the same thing happen to her second. That little girl in there was going to recover. He would allow no other settlement.

He slewed his gaze over to where the curtain drawn hastily across the cubicle where Fern was being examined had snagged at one corner against a chair. It permitted him just enough of a view to see the intravenous solution dripping into her arm, the tube feeding oxygen through her nostrils. She looked pale, but she was breathing on her own, and that, as he well knew, was a good sign.

Only then did he become aware of the hard lump of tension easing in his own chest. What a lovely child she was! If only Sharon would let him, he could love both mother and daughter so easily.

Perplexed, dismayed, he backed away from that thought. How the hell had those two momentous little words, 'If only', slipped by his guard, not to mention the implications that came with them? His mission was to find freedom for his heart, not fetter it more securely in captivity. Compassion he could afford, but love?

'Mr McClure? I'm Barbara Palliser, the attending physician for your daughter.'

Clint looked up at the woman who came to a stop beside them. 'I'm not the husband,' he said, battered by another wave of shock at the realisation that he hated the fact that Sharon no longer bore his name. 'I'm just a friend of the family.' He indicated Sharon. 'This is Fern's mother.'

The sound of a stranger's voice penetrated Sharon's distress. She raised her head. Her lovely green eyes were dazed with grief and worry. 'Fern...?' she breathed on a creaky whisper, as though her throat were raw.

'She's responding well to medication, Mrs McClure.'

'But is she out of danger?' Clint asked, aware that such reassurance was the only thing that would temper Sharon's anguish and make it bearable.

The semi-evasive reply enraged him. 'She's suffering a very severe allergic reaction to wasp venom,' the good doctor hedged.

If she adds that the patient's doing as well as can be expected, Clint thought savagely, I'm going to lose it and say something socially unacceptable that will probably get me booted out of here and do Sharon no damn good at all!

Either Barbara Palliser was a mother herself or she possessed telepathic powers, because she went on to offer a much more satisfactory prognosis. 'But yes, she's out of danger and we have every reason to expect she'll make a full recovery, Mrs McClure. We'd like to keep her overnight for observation, though.'

'But other people's children get stung all the time, and they don't have to be hospitalised,' Sharon protested, shaking her head in the same bewildered way that people caught in the middle of a battle zone were apt to do. Disbelieving; almost catatonic.

'When they respond as your daughter did, they certainly do,' Dr Palliser assured her. 'I gather this is the first time she's been stung, or you'd already know that. Hers isn't the usual localised painful swelling that most people suffer with an insect bite, but a systemic reaction that is extremely dangerous—what we call anaphylactic shock. It can be fatal, Mrs McClure, and you'll have to make sure she carries an anti-venom kit with her all the time from now on, in case she gets stung again.'

It was too much for her to take in, coming so soon after that nightmare drive to get here. Clint thought Sharon was going to keel over. Her face turned ashen and, if her eyes had been huge before, they seemed to double in size, dwarfing her face.

'You were right,' she said, turning her horrified gaze on him. 'You saved her life, Clint.'

The doctor nodded. 'Yes, he did.'

'And now I'm going to save yours,' he said, pulling Sharon to her feet. 'I'm taking you home. You're exhausted.'

'Good.' The doctor offered a brief, sympathetic smile. 'We don't have too many emergency booths in a hospital this size, and you do look about ready to collapse, Mrs McClure. Check with us in the morning and we'll let you know when you can come and get your daughter.'

'I want to see Fern *now*,' Sharon announced. 'I want to see for myself that she's going to be all right.'

'Of course.' Dr Palliser nodded. 'But just for a couple of minutes. Come with me.'

Clint wasn't sure if the permission extended to him, too, but Sharon clutched his hand so tightly that he had little choice but to accompany her to Fern's bedside.

Sensing their presence, the child opened her eyes and offered a sweet, sleepy smile that almost tore his heart out. Who wouldn't love her?

Her mother bent over her, crooning softly. He watched for a little while, until Fern drifted back to sleep, then touched Sharon on the shoulder. 'Time for you to get some rest, too, Sharon.'

She straightened and turned to face him, the tears shimmering. 'I'm staying here,' she quavered—predictably enough, Clint supposed, given her almost obsessive concern for Fern even when the child was well.

But if she didn't recognise how close to breakdown she was, he did, and he'd had enough medical emergencies for one night. 'No, you're not,' he informed her, with the sort of autocratic determination he'd used when airlifting shell-shocked refugees to safety, and led her firmly out of the cubicle. 'I'm quite prepared to carry you out of here if I have to, but I will not let you spend the night on a vinyl couch in a hospital waiting-room, not when you've got a perfectly good bed back at the Dunns'.'

She opened her mouth to argue, but he stopped her by raising his hand point-duty-officer-fashion. 'That's the way it's going to be, Sharon, so save the objections.'

And just to demonstrate that he was quite willing to back up the threat with action, he swung her off her feet and into his arms.

She sagged against him, most of the fight going out of her. 'I don't want to go to the Dunns',' she said in a surprisingly meek voice.

'Why not?'

'Mrs Dunn will never forgive me for stealing the limelight on Margot's wedding-day.'

'The reception's only half over. Vera Dunn is still holding court at the country club and probably not even aware of our little drama.'

'I still don't want to go back to her house. Sooner or later, someone is sure to tell her that Fern's had an accident, and I'm not up to being reproached for having allowed a minor player to upstage the bride.'

'You're overreacting. Margot would never look at it that way.'

'Margot wouldn't—but her mother would.'

Clint couldn't suppress a grin. Sharon was right; Vera Dunn could be a real piece of work when she put her mind to it. 'She is about as irritating as a buzz-saw at times,' he agreed, 'so I can't say I blame you for wanting to avoid her. The question is, though, where would you like to stay instead? With all the people staying in town for the wedding, I imagine the hotel is full.'

To his astonishment, Sharon linked both arms around his neck in the first spontaneous gesture of trust she'd shown him thus far. 'I don't want to be alone, Clint. Tonight I need to be with someone who understands.'

Don't read more into that than she intends, Bodine, he warned himself. The woman's at the end of her rope and is looking for a little brotherly comfort. Raging hormones have no place in this little scenario. 'No problem,' he said, with a good deal more equanimity than he felt. 'The aunts have rooms to spare. You can stay with us.'

The house was just as she remembered it, with down-cushioned window-seats and sofas so soft that a person could sink into them and almost disappear. A huge bouquet of fresh flowers filled the empty hearth in the parlour; bowls of home-made pot-pourri sat on the antique tables. Old photographs of Clint, some going as far back as his babyhood, covered the walls and the top of the spinet piano. The air smelt of lavender and beeswax, and lace curtains hung at the polished panes of the windows.

There was none of the formal splendour of the Dunns' country estate to be found here, nor any of the chic art nouveau elegance of her own parents' city villa, but there was a warmth and comfort that made it a home, right down to the basset hound that ogled her out of amorous, bloodshot eyes. Too large to be a cottage and too small to qualify as a mansion, the aunts' house rambled much like the roses climbing around the covered porch, wandering off into quiet nooks and landings furnished with fat chintz armchairs and reading lamps—quiet places where a person could escape into her own thoughts and be alone without feeling lonely.

It had embraced Sharon ten years ago and it didn't disappoint her now. The minute she walked in the door, she felt the horror of the last two hours begin to recede.

'How about a brandy?' Clint stood in the entrance to the parlour and watched her as she wandered about the room, touching familiar things and renewing herself.

'Actually,' she said, chafing the goose-flesh that crawled over her bare arms, 'what I'd really like to do is get out of these clothes and into something warmer.'

Seed pearls and aquamarine shantung were a fine combination for a wedding, but they didn't lend themselves well to the aftermath of trauma. What she needed was one of Aunt Celeste's hand-quilted robes to erase the chill that had nothing to do with the weather.

Clint was of a similar mind. 'Go soak in a hot bath, then wrap yourself in one of those dressing-gown things that are always kept in the guest-room wardrobe,' he said, waving a hand toward the broad spiral stairway, 'and, while you're gone, I'll fix us a snack. You'll feel better once you eat something.'

'I'm not hungry, and I don't know how you could be, either.'

'Stress gives me an appetite.' He slapped at his flat stomach, as if she needed a reminder that he was as lean and hard today as he had been a decade ago. 'Go on—scoot! Use the blue room; it's got its own bathroom. You remember where it is—to the right of the first landing?'

How could she forget the blue room? It was where she'd spent her wedding night. 'The honeymoon suite', the aunts had called it, clucking and smiling and trying terribly hard to be discreet when she and Clint had finally gone to bed. How were they to guess the bride and groom weren't deliriously happy, or that they made love with the desperation of a couple seeking an escape from disaster?

'I remember,' she said.

Nothing had changed. The same four-poster bed, its rich cherrywood finish gleaming, stood in the middle of the room, covered with the same puffy blue quilt. The heirloom rocking-chair, the mahogany chiffonier, the narrow cheval mirror, each was in exactly the same spot it had occupied ten summers ago.

The bath-tub was the old-fashioned cast-iron kind, with claw feet and huge brass taps. Deep enough for a person to be able to immerse herself up to the chin, it had been designed by someone who understood the therapeutic powers of warm, scented water.

Clint was mistaken on one point, however. There weren't any quilted robes hanging in the wardrobe, when she went looking, but there was a smocked white cotton nightdress, ornately embroidered with pale blue forget-me-nots and so thoroughly Victorian in style that nothing but her hands and feet showed when Sharon slipped it on.

Pulling aside the curtains, she opened the little bedroom window tucked under the gables and leaned on the ledge, surprised to find that only a pale orange glow remained of the sunset. Enough of the day's heat lingered, though, to perfume the evening with night-scented stock and honeysuckle, just as it had on her wedding night. Tucking her feet under her, she sank down into the rocking-chair, and breathed in the fragrance. And the memories came flooding back...

What had prompted her mother to give her a négligé as a trousseau gift? Some last-minute pang of guilt or regret, perhaps, that she hadn't made more of an effort to provide her only child with the traditional trappings a bride might expect? Or some misguided hope that, if the package were glamorised a little, the groom might be tempted to overlook the fact that he'd been railroaded into marriage? Whatever the reason, Sharon had felt ridiculous in the ruffled Hollywood creation, and hadn't worn it. Hers had not been a champagne and roses sort of honeymoon; it had been a 'let's make the best of it' period of adjustment and re-evaluation.

The day after the wedding, they'd moved a few blocks away to the lower floor of a house that had been converted into two apartments. The day after that, Clint had packed a bag with enough clothes to last him a week and had gone out with the local land surveyor, who'd hired him as his assistant to subdivide recreational lakefront property in the mountains a hundred and fifty miles north of town. 'I've got to make a living somehow,' he'd said brusquely, when she'd voiced her dismay at his proposed five-day absences.

She'd had three rooms to clean and more hours than she cared to count in which to dwell on her misery. On the other hand, the couple in the upstairs apartment, who were also newly-weds, were true honeymooners. Their bed had creaked and groaned every night in testimony of their wedded bliss, while she lay lonely in hers and cried into her pillow.

In some ways, the weekends were even worse. She'd been hopelessly in love with Clint, and it had hurt her terribly to see the desolation in his eyes when he came home each Friday, and to know that she was the reason for it. He hadn't taken the job in order to be able to pay the rent, as he'd claimed. He had a degree in political science and could have found more lucrative employment closer to home. No, he'd taken the job to leave himself too physically spent to care about the ambitions he'd had to abandon when he'd done the honourable thing and married her.

Despite his exhaustion, though, she knew he'd often lain awake beside her at night, staring at the darkened ceiling, and she'd felt his remoteness. Sometimes he'd reach for her and they'd make love silently and economically. But although he'd occasionally share his body, he never shared his soul, and she had known better than to ask him for his heart.

He was separate from her, even when they were physically joined. She'd never felt that she was able to touch him, except in the most superficial sense.

After a couple of weeks she'd decided that she had to keep herself occupied or she'd go mad, so during the days she'd started to garden. There were whole beds of neglected roses and lilacs, delphiniums and phlox, which needed weeding and pruning, and a patch of lawn to be trimmed. In the evenings she'd painted the rooms and tried to make the apartment a cheerful, welcoming place that he'd be glad to come home to.

And then, one night, she'd woken up and found she'd started bleeding. By the time Clint had come home three days later, it was all over—or so she'd thought—and too late to save their baby or their marriage. They'd been left with nothing but recriminations that had them hurling damaging, hurtful accusations at each other across an abyss of sadness.

'Why couldn't you have waited for me to help you with the damned garden?'

'Because you're not interested in helping me. You're never here when I need you. It's your fault I lost the baby.'

'Always assuming you were pregnant to begin with! How do I know that wasn't just another one of your ploys to get me to marry you?'

There'd been nothing left after that except the sudden opening of doors that they thought had been shut forever. She'd sensed his impatience to be free of the legalities that still tied him to her, and for the first time was able to offer him something that really mattered: his freedom.

She had agreed to a speedy divorce. Within a week he had left Canada.

He might have dropped off the edge of the earth for all she'd heard from him after that. If she'd had the slightest inkling that he'd come looking for her one day, she might have made a different decision that day in the doctor's office, about six weeks after he disappeared. But he'd sent no messages, no letters, and her sorrow had eroded to bitter resentment.

She had decided she hated him. It had been so much less painful than admitting she loved him. And when she'd learned that she'd conceived fraternal twins and lost only one of them, she'd hoarded the knowledge and told herself that the surviving baby was better off with no father at all than with one who'd been so reluctant to accept the role in the first place. And in the years that followed, life had slowly regained a measure of sweetness.

Music drifted up the stairs, something calm and restful by Debussy. The notes fell like small round pebbles into a quiet pond, so gentle that they scarcely caused a ripple.

Sharon leaned back in the rocking-chair and closed her eyes, thinking about that other child. It wasn't something she often did—ten years was a long time to keep such a tenuous memory alive—but every once in a while she found herself wondering: had it been a boy or a girl? Would it have resembled her, as Fern did, or would it have looked like Clint?

At first he paid no attention to the fact that she was taking so long. He changed from the formal rented suit to a blue shirt and denim jeans as soft and comfortable as a pair of old slippers, then called the hospital to check on Fern and left the aunts' phone number in case some change in her condition occurred. He sliced tomatoes and carved wafer-thin slices of honey-cured ham. His aunts weren't great imbibers of alcohol, but Jubilee made a mean apricot brandy that went very well with coffee, and there was half a damson pie in the refrigerator just begging to be served up with a dollop of ice-cream.

When he glanced at the schoolhouse clock on the kitchen wall, saw that an hour had passed, and realised that if Sharon was still upstairs she was awfully quiet, he decided to go looking for her. He didn't like the disappointment that washed over him at the idea that she might have skipped out on him.

There was no light showing under the guest-room door, no sound of running water to indicate that she might still be in the bath-tub. Very quietly, he turned the knob and inched the door ajar.

He saw her at once, huddled in the rocking-chair with the folds of her gown spilling around her ankles and trailing to the floor. Her face was bathed in faint starlight, just enough for him to see tear tracks silvering her cheeks and the fact that she was crying in her sleep.

Perhaps a floorboard creaked under his feet. More likely, though, he let out a groan at the sight of her, because her pain or grief immediately became his, too.

Why was that? Had the habit of shouldering responsibility for others become too much a part of his life for him to react any other way? Or was it simply an extension of the guilt he'd nursed for so long—the automatic assumption that if she was suffering it was his fault?

No matter. Something disturbed her. She awoke with a jolt, sat upright in the old rocker, and swung her head blindly to where he stood in the doorway, haloed by the light in the hall behind him. 'What...?'

'Sorry,' he said. 'I didn't mean to startle you. I came to make sure you were OK, that's all. You were gone rather a long time.'

The alarm drained out of her. 'I was dreaming,' she said, pressing her fingertips to her temples.

'It must have been a nightmare.' He stepped cautiously over the threshold, unsure of his welcome. 'You were crying.'

'So I was.' She wiped absently at her cheeks.

'Were you dreaming about Fern? I checked with the hospital a few minutes ago and she's doing just fine.'

'No,' Sharon said. 'I was dreaming about her——'

The words choked off abruptly, smothered by the hand she clapped to her mouth. She turned huge, horrified eyes towards him.

It happened again then, that slamming pain in his midriff, so much stronger this time that he felt driven to act on it. Unable to stop himself, he plucked her bodily from the chair so that he could sit in it himself and snuggle her on his lap.

'Dreaming about what, darling?' he crooned softly. 'Why don't you tell me? Talking often helps, and I'm a good listener.'

She froze in his arms, appalled at what she'd almost confessed. Would he have been as anxious to comfort her if she'd finished what she'd started to say—that she'd been dreaming about Fern's twin? She wished she had the courage to find out.

'Your being here helps,' she said, and in a way it was true. It felt right to be close to him like this. The secret of Fern's paternity lay between them like a land-mine primed to explode, but not even that could blind her to the knowledge that the more time she spent with him, the easier it became to understand why she'd fallen headlong in love with him in the first place.

Was that what prompted the insidious notion that, given more favourable circumstances, those early feelings could mature into something more substantial than so much adolescent stardust? 'Talk to me instead,' she begged, squashing the thought before it incurred fresh disaster and heartache. 'Tell me what you did after the divorce.'

'Why dredge up the unhappy past when the present is so much more relevant?' he asked, running a warm, dry palm down her arm until he found her hand.

'Because I'm missing a whole piece of your life and I can't help being curious about what you did with it. You aren't the same man I once knew, and I want to know what changed you.'

Time had mellowed Clint. The wicked sense of fun that had first attracted her to him had re-established itself as a permanent part of his personality, in charming contrast to his strong and sober sense of purpose. He'd matured into a man at last in control of every facet of his life, and perhaps this afforded him a more indulgent outlook on the rest of the world, but during the few short weeks of their marriage he'd shown little tolerance, either for himself or for others. He'd been like a caged animal, searching for an avenue of escape. His frustration at not finding one had simmered so close to the surface that she'd been almost afraid of him at times.

'Are you disappointed at what I've become? Is that it?' he asked her now.

Would that she were! How much easier it would be to resist him then. 'No. I'm just curious.' She wriggled more snugly against his shoulder and allowed her fingers to curl around his. 'Where did you go when you left this country?'

He laughed. 'You're a bit old for bedtime stories, dear heart, but I'll humour you, just this once. My first stop was India.'

She'd always seen him as some sort of modern-day crusader, fighting other people's wars for the thrill of it and covering himself with glory in the process, yet India didn't seem a very likely place for such adventures. 'What did you do there?'

'Drove an old mail truck back and forth across the country, collecting waifs and orphans and delivering them to hostels, where they were taken care of until such time as better arrangements could be made for them.'

'You must have found that very satisfying.'

'I suppose I did, to begin with, but I soon became frustrated by the limitations I faced every day. Speed makes all the difference when it comes to saving lives, and that old truck was always breaking down. I had to find a quicker, more efficient method of getting around, so I learned to fly fixed-wing aircraft, then joined forces with an Australian guy who flew helicopters. Between us we covered a lot more territory and had some pretty hair-raising experiences along the way.'

'How long did you stay?'

'A couple of years. Eventually there were enough people involved for the project to win government backing, so we moved on to fresh adventures.'

His voice reminded her of velvet drawn repeatedly over silk, slightly rough without being at all ungentle, and pleasurably hypnotic. His thumb stroked absently past the elastic hem of her sleeve to trace circles over her inner wrist. The night could have been forty hours long and she would not have tired of listening to him or being touched by him. 'Where did you go next?'

'Africa—Ethiopia and Nigeria—then South America. Paraguay, Bolivia, Brazil.' His tone changed, grew darker and more distant. 'And it was the same thing everywhere. Men killing each other, people starving, children dying. And fools like me who deluded themselves into thinking they could make a difference.'

'Don't say that,' she protested. 'What you did helped.'

'It didn't amount to a row of beans. People continued to starve and children continued to die, sometimes violently and always tragically. Those children...' His voice was suddenly raw with anguish. 'I sometimes think the faces of those children will follow me to my grave.'

It was her turn to offer comfort, and it took only a very small movement for her to lift her head and press her lips to his cheek. 'Their lives were made better for having known you, Clint.'

'Was yours?' he asked in a low voice, turning his face so that his mouth was close to hers.

He was looking at her. She could see the faint gleam of the stars reflecting in his eyes. She felt the intensity of his gaze, heard the plea in his words, and for once it was easy to be honest with him. 'Yes,' she whispered. 'Oh, yes...' You taught me how to love!

Her answer died on a sigh that became hopelessly tangled against his lips. She didn't know who initiated the kiss, nor did she care at first. She was far too occupied returning in full measure the demands his mouth was making on hers. Her arms tightened around his neck, her head fell back against his shoulder, and if the rocking-chair wasn't meant for two it wasn't designed for secrets, either. She knew very well the impact of that kiss on him.

'What were we talking about?' he whispered, necklacing kisses from one corner of her mouth to the other like so many pearls on a string.

Keep your wits about you and watch what you say, she told herself sternly, but her brain ignored her and joined forces with her racing heart. 'How much better my life has been because of you,' she said, the words exacting a terrible outlay of energy as they stumbled from her mouth.

'I fail to see how,' Clint murmured, untying the ribbons at her throat.

She ought to distract him, find some way to stop him. She'd already allowed him too much latitude, and if she let him touch her more intimately she'd be lost and have no one but herself to blame for the outcome. To indulge the craving for him that she'd suffered almost from the moment she'd set eyes on him again was pure madness.

She sat up and pushed away his hands. 'You haven't mentioned anything about other women in your life,' she said bluntly, seizing on the one topic guaranteed to sour the intimacy of the moment.

He grew very still. 'Ah, so it's the women I've known that you really want to hear about,' he said softly, a slow smile glimmering over his mouth.

'Well, unless you spent the last ten years in a monastery, you must have known some,' she said, wishing she hadn't brought up the subject, because, far from defusing her aching desire, she'd merely fuelled it with jealousy.

'Do you mean in the biblical sense, dear heart?' he enquired mischievously.

She twisted the ribbons of her gown between her fingers and tried to look blasé. 'Naturally,' she said, sounding commendably bored.

He leaned his head against the high back of the rocker and rested his hands along its arms. 'Well, let me see, there were Fatima and Salome in Egypt...and then there was Carmen in Argentina, and after her came Scheherazade in Arabia.' He rolled his eyes until the whites gleamed in the dark. 'Scheherazade,' he murmured, practically licking his lips, 'was quite fantastic.'

'I'm sure she was,' Sharon said waspishly, 'but I really don't want a list of names and addresses of your many conquests.'

He sat up straight, setting the chair to a wild rocking. 'What do you want, then? To hear that I remained faithful to you, even though you upped and married another man before the sheets were cold from my sleeping in them?'

'I was just wondering in general because it seemed time to change the subject,' she said, shrivelling under his attack. 'Did you—er—did you really know a Scheherazade?'

'No.' He sighed with a trace of his old impatience. 'Nor did I know a Fatima or Carmen or Salome. But there were other women.'

'Oh,' she said in a small voice, and wished he didn't always feel compelled to be so damned forthright with his answers.

'If you didn't want to know, you shouldn't have asked,' he chided. 'If, on the other hand, what you're really asking is if they had any lasting significance in my life, then the answer is no.'

'But you made love to them,' she said, deciding that when it came to self-flagellation she deserved first prize.

'In certain situations,' Clint said, with strained forbearance. 'For example, in extreme danger—the sort where you can't be at all sure you won't wake up dead the next morning—people tend to turn to each other. On occasion, there were women, Sharon, to whom I turned. You might choose to interpret that as my having used them. I saw it as a mutual and generous exchange of comfort.'

She had no warning of what her next words would be. They popped out before she had the chance to silence them. 'Did you ever think of me when you were with them?'

'Frequently. Are you satisfied, or are there more crazy questions where that one came from?'

'No more questions,' she said.

He cupped her cheek in his hand and turned her mouth to his. 'Then I have a question for you.'

'And what's that?' she asked nervously.

'Why do you care?'

When she needed it the most, her ability to prevaricate deserted her. 'I don't know,' she whispered.

He tilted up her chin. 'I do,' he said, kissing her throat. 'It's because you don't want anyone else to come between us, especially not now. It's because you want it to be just the two of us, here and now, on that bed over there. Not because we're surrounded by danger or threats from outside, but because that old magic is working for us again, whether you want to admit it or not.'

CHAPTER EIGHT

CLINT'S mouth singed where it touched, the flame spreading down into her lungs and parching as it went. 'Am I right?' he murmured.

'What...?'

'You heard me.'

She swallowed twice. 'I—er—I...'

'A simple yes or no will do.' He lifted his head and trailed the fingers of each hand down the sides of her neck until they formed a V at the open ribbons of her nightgown. 'But you do have to answer me, Sharon, and you do have to tell the truth.'

If ever a lie was justified, it was then, but she couldn't voice it. His eyes held hers and compelled her to honesty. 'Yes,' she said, on the merest whisper of a breath.

He nodded and expelled a long sigh. 'Yes,' he echoed and, carrying her to the bed, laid her against the pillows and looked down at her face for a long time without touching her. 'Oh, yes!'

Very deliberately then, he bent and kissed the corner of her mouth, pushed aside the ribbons of her gown, and touched his lips to the spot where her pulse quivered with the frantic, uneven flutter of a captured butterfly.

Behind him, the lamp at the top of the stairs spilled a beam of light across the wall, a plea for discretion before they sank into bewitchment. 'The door...' she

123

protested, jerking her head towards it. 'What if your aunts...?'

Lifting his head, Clint glanced over his shoulder and cursed softly. 'That would never do,' he agreed, reluctantly leaving her side to remedy the situation.

To her relief, closing the door plunged the room into near-darkness. She was just able to discern him moving to the foot of the bed. She heard the tell-tale clink of a belt buckle, the soft hiss of a zip. His clothes hit the floor with a quiet thud, and then he moved away, towards the high chiffonier. For one insane moment Sharon wondered if, overcome by uncharacteristic modesty, he was looking for pyjamas or something.

The scrape and flare of a match disabused her of any such notion. Yellow candlelight chased the shadows to the corners of the room and showed him silhouetted against the wall. He was not wearing pyjamas. He was not wearing anything. He was stalking back to the bed, stark naked.

Sharon promptly shut her eyes, overcome by a tidal wave of shyness. Making love in the semi-dark was one thing; clearly seeing and being seen was quite another.

'Open your eyes, dear heart,' he said, his raspy, sexy voice seeming to reach out to stroke over her as the mattress sank under his weight.

Reluctantly she did. He loomed above her, large, powerful, intimidating. 'That's better,' he said.

With excruciating delicacy his fingers skimmed from her throat to her feet and grasped the hem of her gown. Then they began the journey back, but slowly this time, pleating the fabric as they went.

He uncovered her ankles, lifted them, and dipped his head to bestow a long, slow kiss on each instep. The reverberations shot the length of her, shaking her to the roots of the hair on her head.

He bared her calves and traced their curve with his tongue. Her knees fell apart, slack with invitation, but he was bent on a more leisurely seduction. Declining to accept, he pressed them together and fanned his breath over her thigh to that demure sweep of skin that really did nothing more than join a woman's leg to the rest of her body. Not a secret place, to be kept hidden from all but a lover's eyes, but one she exposed without shame when she wore a swimsuit. Yet when Clint found it and stopped to test its resilience with quick, light flicks of his tongue, it shed all pretence of innocence and responded with a volatile humming that elicited a moan of startled pleasure from Sharon.

He pushed the gown higher, followed it with his mouth. He looped her waist with kisses, counted each rib with his tongue, swirled his mouth over the slope of her breasts. The flame leapt more fiercely.

'Give me your hand,' he commanded, his voice rustling over her like dry leaves.

She obeyed, completely at his mercy. He pulled the sleeve of her gown free, then followed suit with the other. Last, he lifted the garment clear of her head and left her fully uncovered, then let his eyes roam over her in a ritual of renewal that left her trembling.

Her nineteen-year-old body had been the lure that had tempted and trapped him before. Would it betray her now? She was almost thirty, and the signs were there for anyone who chose to look for them: the breasts not quite as firm and high, the hips a little rounder, the waist never again as slender as it had been before childbirth. Would he notice? Would he compare? And if he saw the changes, would he still want her?

She squirmed, afraid to look him in the eye, afraid that uncompromising honesty of his would not allow him to dissemble at what he saw.

'Be still,' he growled, and to ensure that she obeyed he took her wrists and held them above her head. Pinned beneath him, she had no choice but to submit as he set about a scrupulous examination of discovery. He did not miss an inch and he would not be hurried. She felt stripped to the soul and mortally vulnerable under that fine and lingering scrutiny.

When at last he spoke, it was merely to repeat that same, gravelly 'Yes!', but it told her volumes, as did his heavy-lidded gaze. Whatever else he might be feeling, it wasn't disappointment.

The knowledge sparked a tiny courage in her that freed her to return the favour. She dared to look—at his shoulders, his arms, his chest—and discovered that he was as powerfully lean and beautiful at thirty-eight as he had been in his twenties.

Growing braver, she allowed her gaze to slide down the tapering line of his torso, past the flat plane of his stomach to his neat and narrow waist. And then she threw all caution to the windless night, dipped her eyes lower still, and saw that he was not nearly as reconciled to patient seduction as she'd first thought, but was waging a terrible battle to hold himself in check.

It gave her confidence an enormous boost. Very gently she slipped her wrist free of his hold and pressed her hand to his skull, imprisoning him against her.

Desire hammered at him, an exquisite, unrelenting torture screaming for an appeasement he would not grant. In the past it seemed he had always made love to her hastily, in the dark, either because instant gratification had seemed crucial to survival, or because night hid the quiet desperation he knew lurked in her eyes.

But if he retained no clear memory of how she'd looked at nineteen, he knew he would never forget the woman lying beneath him now, with the light from the candle painting her in translucent colour.

Had his bride been as lovely as this exquisite stranger with skin as warm as sun-kissed peaches and as silky as cream? She had *felt* different then, that much he did know. She'd been a girl, lovely in the way that early spring was lovely, on the brink of unfolding, fresh and untouched. But she was all woman now, her early promise of beauty in full bloom and spiced with mystery and allure.

He wanted to taste every inch of her and kiss every curve. He wanted to know her, really know her, to delve below her elegant surface to the complex grace of her soul. And most of all, he wanted the thrill of discovery to last beyond the moment.

He settled his mouth again on her breast and found her nipple ripe and ready for him. A distant tremor seized her, like the far-off warning of an earthquake, fire beneath the cool ice of her reserve.

Her breath fluttered light and rapid in her throat. Blindly she reached for him. 'Let me touch you,' she begged, pushing persuasively at his chest. He rolled on to his back, intrigued and delighted by her sudden aggression.

But the intrigue soon died and the delight thickened to a painful intensity. Her fingers were nimble as humming-birds, their erotic promise devising tortures he'd never imagined. When she lifted her head and closed her mouth on his bare chest, his heart gave a great thudding heave, then seemed to stop. Its dying echo left him too stunned to prepare himself for her next attack.

She nibbled at his shoulder, stroked her tongue up his throat, then lifted her head and smiled into his eyes. 'That's better,' she said.

He'd sadly underestimated the opposition! 'Better for whom?' he croaked, deciding that immediate retaliatory action was called for if he seriously wanted to prolong the pleasure of the moment. Cupping the back of her head, he brought her mouth down hard on his, seeking to disarm her with a kiss entirely dedicated to imitating the act of love.

It was a fine idea except that it backfired. Her lips opened in welcome, deluding him into believing that he was in control and she merely complying with his demands. But honey had never tasted sweeter, and sampling it once wasn't enough. He probed deeper, and never noticed that the doors to escape had closed behind him until it was too late and she was wreaking a devastation of her own beside which his meagre attack paled.

In the full knowledge that he was completely distracted and unable to defend himself elsewhere, she set about enslaving him completely. Her hands, cool and soft as a breeze, shaped his waist and smoothed down his hips, turned hot, possessive vixen, and closed over him. And if that weren't penalty enough to teach any man a lesson, she laughed low in her throat, a sound so utterly female and full of promise that, if she'd asked him for the moon in exchange for making love with him, he'd have used the stars as stepping-stones to get it for her.

Only one thing saved him: the knowledge that if he didn't wrest control away from her the pleasure would end too soon. With an agility that cost him dearly and took her completely by surprise, he rolled her over until she was lying beside him.

'My turn,' he whispered hoarsely, and set about teaching her a lesson he didn't intend she would soon forget.

He kissed her, then he kissed her again. He slid both arms around her and pinned her beneath him, and kissed her a third time, a long, warm, open-mouthed, delicious kiss. And all the time his hands shaped her, coaxing, tormenting, cajoling.

He was more daring than she. Where his hands went, his mouth followed, leaving in their wake an involuntary trembling she could not subdue.

She sighed his name, and she whimpered for him to stop, and she very charmingly begged him not to. And when she melted, helpless to prevent her throbbing capitulation to his attack, he tried to smile in victory and found he couldn't. Her eyes, limpid and unfocused, were utterly defenceless, killing any pretence of laughter in him and evoking instead a feeling dangerously close to love.

There was no more delaying. He wasn't made of stone, after all. Bracing himself on his forearms, he held her face between his hands, nudged apart her thighs, and sank into her. Her hips melted against his, begging outrageously. She was all satin acceptance, tight and welcoming, and she almost destroyed him. For one brief, terrible moment, desire clutched at him so relentlessly that he thought it would all be over before he could begin to give her one tenth of the pleasure she had already afforded him.

He froze, buried his face in her hair, and recited the days of the week in a litany of devout concentration, drawing in a great gasp of gratitude when the delaying tactic took some effect.

After perhaps thirty seconds, he moved very cautiously. She responded, the lovely aching rhythm meshing as though they'd rehearsed together for years. She looked up at him, and her gaze was clear and unafraid. For the first time they were truly united with no secrets between them.

Inevitably, the tempo increased. Passion shimmered, expectant, tantalising. Again he sought to delay. If it had been in his power, he would never have let it end.

'I want you to know,' he murmured, looking deep into her beautiful eyes, 'that those other women...' He paused, dragged a breath from deep down in his lungs to fortify himself against the grabbing hunger. 'They meant nothing, Sharon.'

'Please...' she whispered, her fingers digging into the flesh of his shoulder.

He thought she was trying to silence him, but he had to go on; he had to tell her that this time was like no other. He couldn't let her believe that for him it was just another release. 'They were substitutes for the real thing, dear heart.'

He heard his voice from a growing distance, wavering, wrestling, losing the battle. It might have been the first time since the last time he'd held her. It *was* the first time he'd made love in ten years.

'This,' he whispered hoarsely, 'is for all those nights when I let you lie lonely beside me.'

He felt her tighten around him. 'Oh, please,' she begged, hopelessness swimming in her voice, 'please don't make me love you again.'

So help him, he couldn't resist the lure of her sweet, soft lips or the words they were uttering. Dropping his mouth hard on hers, he set about releasing all the fire simmering within her.

She gasped, convulsed around him. Melted and convulsed, over and over. And he was lost, his control shot to hell and his determination to make this moment last fragmented by that old, relentless hunger that he'd tried for so long to ignore. It didn't matter how many women he'd kissed since the divorce, or how many had shared his bed, his nights.

It didn't matter and it didn't help. Covering her with unplanned, frantic kisses that missed as often as they found their mark, he dissolved into a brilliant, blinding shaking apart—a dissolution of the man he'd become into something eternal and beautiful because he was with her. 'Why can't I make you love me again, my darling?' he whispered, between heaving, jagged breaths. '*You've* bewitched *me* again.'

It had never been this way with Jason, Sharon thought dimly, fighting to snatch oxygen from the place where her lungs used to be. Never such complete surrender, never such astounding passion, never such brutal release as she found with Clint.

It did no good to tell herself that he spelled danger, that that pagan sensuality of his was coupled with an intellect so acute that he would never allow a romantic interlude to cloud his judgement. It didn't seem to matter that tomorrow, when the cool head of reason again prevailed, the ramifications of tonight's events would turn the rest of her life into a shambles.

What mattered was that Clint's arms were around her, holding her safe until the shattered parts of her reassembled themselves. What mattered was that, just once, he had made love to her, instead of having sex. She would not reproach herself for her weakness, or fret at how different things might have been had Fern been conceived in such a manner. She would allow nothing else to intrude until she had crystallised this night in her memory so that it would remain clear and strong for the rest of her life.

He wasn't there when she awoke the next morning, but Aunt Celeste was. She shuffled to the bedside with a tea tray in her hands. 'Darling girl...' She beamed when Sharon opened sleepy eyes. 'How lovely it is to see you back in our home again!'

Sharon shrank under the covers, mortified by the nightgown lying in a heap on the floor. Her lips felt crushed, her face rosy with whisker burn. Her body ached pleasurably. She might as well have worn a placard around her neck, advertising the events of last night.

'How did you know I was here?' she mumbled, then wondered if there were any other dopey questions where that one came from.

'Clinton told us at breakfast.'

'You've had breakfast already? I wish you'd woken me. I need to phone the hospital about Fern.'

'Clinton already did, and she's just fine. You can pick her up any time you're ready, but he left strict instructions that you weren't to be disturbed before ten—said you underwent quite an ordeal last night, you poor thing, and that you'd earned your rest.'

The rat! They'd made love until the sun came up, snatching sleep in each other's arms until the breathtaking hunger brought them together again. Small wonder she felt limp as a rag doll.

Aunt Celeste patted her cheek lovingly. 'I brewed you raspberry tea, darling. So restorative, I always find, when a person's had a hard night of it. Come down as soon as you're dressed. Jubilee has made you waffles for breakfast.'

Immediately she was alone, Sharon leapt from the bed and raced to the mirror. What she saw staring back at her was every bit as bad as she'd feared: the face of a woman half dazed with love. Starry-eyed, sultry, sated. She had to erase the look, and quickly.

Within ten minutes she had showered and scrambled into her clothes. Fully dressed, she felt much more in command of herself.

Jubilee Bodine might have been harder of hearing than her sister, but she compensated by being much more observant. 'My gracious, child,' she declared, snapping closed the lid of the waffle iron and turning a shrewd eye her way as Sharon slid on to the chair in the breakfast nook of the big kitchen, 'you look no more rested than Our Boy this morning. What's the matter—couldn't the pair of you sleep?'

Sharon choked on the orange juice Celeste had poured for her. 'I... Yes—um—very well... We...' She sputtered, coughed, and proceeded to reduce herself to total absurdity. 'We—had—a wonderful—er...'

'Night,' Aunt Jubilee finished for her. 'Yes, I can tell. Slap her on the back, Celeste, before she has a heart attack.'

Sharon mopped her eyes with her serviette and decided that this was definitely a case of least said, soonest mended. Wily Aunt Jubilee *knew*, which meant that before long she'd apprise Celeste of the situation, too. Afraid to look either of them in the eye, Sharon stared out of the window.

'Cat got your tongue?' Aunt Jubilee enquired archly, setting peach syrup and fresh cream on the table.

Sharon searched for some scintillating reply. 'I was admiring the pink rose in the garden,' she offered weakly. 'See how lovely it looks with the dew still on it?'

'You sound like something out of a child's first reader,' Jubilee pronounced. '"Oh, oh, see Spot run! See Sharon run! See Sharon pretend she doesn't want to know where Clinton is!"' She cackled with malicious delight. 'Pour the girl some coffee, Celeste. It might restore her wits.'

'Don't tease her, Jubilee!' Celeste scolded, slip-slopping in her large, comfortable slippers across the kitchen floor. 'Her little daughter's in the hospital and she's worried.'

'I know that.' Jubilee deposited a plate heaped with golden waffles in front of Sharon. 'One of the joys of passing eighty is being able to say what you please without getting rapped on the knuckles for it, so save your breath, Sister. Sharon ought to know by now that I've always loved her.' She fixed Sharon in another piercing gaze and smiled slyly. 'Eat, child, before you wilt. You need to replenish your energy.'

'How was the rest of the wedding?' Sharon asked, determined to steer the conversation to less suggestive channels. 'I'm afraid we missed quite a lot of it.'

'Lovely,' Aunt Celeste sighed. 'Simply lovely!'

'Ostentatious,' Jubilee said, 'although I have to say, your gowns were quite beautiful, Sharon. Margot did look exquisite—but then so did you.'

Celeste nodded. 'And little Fern. What a shame the day was spoiled for her.'

'What a blessing Clinton was there,' Jubilee said.

'Yes.' Sharon leapt at the chance to steer the conversation to a mutually acceptable topic. 'I was so impressed at the way he took charge. He guessed right away what had happened and seemed to know exactly what to do.'

'Well, of course he did!' Jubilee exclaimed. 'He's had enough practice, after all.'

'He's allergic to bee-stings, too,' Celeste added, seeing Sharon's puzzled frown. 'He always had to carry a little anti-venom kit with him when he was a boy.'

'Still does,' Jubilee said. 'Especially with him spending so much time in foreign places where they have all sorts of biting insects no right-minded man would want to associate with.'

The waffles were delicious, the coffee strong and flavourful. Sharon had been on the verge of relaxing until this last little titbit of information was dropped in her lap. She could almost feel herself turn pale. 'Clint is allergic to bee-stings?' she repeated. 'I didn't know that.'

'You would have if you'd been around him when he was little, dear girl,' Celeste said, refilling her coffee-cup. 'Children seem to have a talent for stumbling on nests in the most unlikely places.'

'Fern's never been stung before,' Sharon said.

'That's because she's a little city girl,' Celeste replied comfortably. 'They don't go climbing trees and exploring in the bushes the way little boys in the country do. Why, it seems to me that hardly a day went by when Clint was young that he didn't stumble on a nest of one kind or another. We got very used to coping with emergencies.' She stirred her coffee meditatively. 'It's quite a coincidence, when you stop to think about it, that Fern should suffer from the same sort of reaction.'

Mindless panic took hold of Sharon. It was the only way she could explain the utter idiocy of her next remark. 'It's not hereditary,' she blurted out, and managed to up-end her cup into its saucer.

Jubilee was looking at her strangely. 'My gracious, Sharon, no one suggested it is.'

'Of course not.' She dabbed agitatedly at a spot of coffee on the embroidered cloth, babbling the whole time. 'It's just that... well, what I meant is that *I'm* not allergic, nor was Jason. I didn't mean...didn't mean...'

Jubilee responded very uncharacteristically to that outpouring of excuses. She patted Sharon's hand. 'No need to explain, dear child,' she remarked gently. 'I understand exactly what you meant.'

Sharon was afraid she did, only too well.

Celeste rose and went over to the china cupboard. 'Let me get you a fresh cup, dear.'

'No, thank you!' Plopping her serviette on the table, Sharon pushed back her chair and tried not to appear too suddenly anxious to be gone. 'It's getting late and I really would like to go back to the Dunns' and change out of this outfit before I pick up Fern.'

'You are dressed rather formally for the morning,' Jubilee acknowledged, with that same enigmatic expression still on her face, 'but if you wait a few more minutes Clinton should be back. He's gone into Harperville to return his rented suit, but I'm sure he'd be only too glad to drive you to the hospital when he gets back.'

That was the last thing Sharon wanted. If Jubilee hadn't already put two and two together and come up with four, she was coming awfully close. The sooner Sharon put some distance—a lot of distance!—between herself and the Bodines, the less chance of her opening her mouth and letting something even more incriminating fall out.

'I couldn't possibly put him to all that trouble,' she said firmly.

'But he'll be disappointed at having missed you,'

Celeste objected. 'Jubilee, persuade her to wait for Clinton.'

'The girl's in a tearing hurry, Sister, as you'd be able to see if you stopped flapping around long enough to take a look. Nevertheless...' Jubilee fastened a severe gaze on Sharon '... he is going to wonder what drove you away so quickly.'

Let him draw whatever conclusions he pleased, Sharon thought. She'd behaved like a complete fool, on a number of counts. As if that defensive gaffe about heredity weren't enough, she'd actually been entertaining romantic fantasies about her and Clint somehow managing to find a happy ending together, when she knew that was something that could never happen. Her deception stood between them. It always would.

She was furious with herself; furious and disgusted. She was no more in touch with reality now than she had been at nineteen if she'd reached the point of deluding herself into believing that she could tell him the truth, then expect that, dazzled by one magical night of love, he'd forgive her.

Not likely, not with the Clint Bodine she knew!

'I have other things that I'd planned to do today as soon as I've picked up Fern,' she told the aunts.

Like catch the noon flight back to Vancouver. She couldn't afford to spend another day—or night—in Crescent Creek.

CHAPTER NINE

VANCOUVER was hot, humid and too crowded after the rural peace of Crescent Creek. Even the penthouse seemed claustrophobic, and Sharon found none of the tranquillity there that usually awaited her after time spent elsewhere. She also knew why. She missed Clint. Desperately.

To make matters worse, Fern talked about him incessantly. He'd become her favourite topic of conversation, and she was disappointed—disturbingly so—at having been whisked back to town before she could say goodbye to him. It was all Sharon could do not to snap back that life would have been a lot simpler if he'd never said hello, either.

Another change of scene seemed like an excellent diversion, both for mother and daughter—something as far removed from reminders of Clint as it was possible to find. 'How would you like to visit Disneyland?' she suggested, two days after they had fled Crescent Creek.

'Disneyland?' Fern's eyes were like saucers. 'Mommy, yes!'

'Then spend the rest of the summer driving up the California coast? We could start in San Diego, take a tour of Hollywood, go to San Francisco, and visit all the mission towns along the way. It's really beautiful down there, sweetheart, and I think you'd have fun.'

'I'd love it, I know I would.'

'We'd get back a few days before school starts, and by then...' Sharon let the words dribble into silence. She could hardly finish what she'd been thinking—that by then she'd have her priorities firmly in place again—without inviting questions she didn't want to answer from her sometimes too perceptive daughter.

But Fern's smile faded a little anyway. 'What's the matter, Mommy? Are you feeling sad again?'

Giving herself a mental shake, Sharon vowed to leave Clint in Crescent Creek, where he belonged, and forge ahead with new places and new experiences. 'Absolutely not.'

But Fern was wise beyond her years. 'Then why are we going away when we only just got home? When you came to get me from the hospital, you said you wanted to get back to Vancouver as fast as you could, and now you want to leave again.'

'You didn't have much of a birthday party this year,' Sharon replied, thinking fast on her feet for a change. 'What with all the work involved in Margot's wedding, your special day got sort of swept under the carpet, so consider this trip a belated celebration. We'll have a wonderful time, I promise.'

And they did. They came back to Vancouver late one afternoon towards the end of the first week of September to find that the enervating heat of summer had passed. Across the Strait, the mountains on the distant islands loomed dusky purple against a sky of clear, cool green, splashed with gold where the sun had gone down. Indian summer had arrived—that marvellous month-long reprieve of crisp mornings, mild, sunny afternoons and cool evenings. Before the cold rains of winter set in, Clint Bodine would be no more than a distant memory. Sharon was convinced of all those things, especially the last.

'As soon as we've unpacked, we'll phone and order in pizza,' she told Fern, drawing up the blinds and flinging open the terrace doors to the cool ocean breeze. 'Then, while you put your room into half-decent order, I'll take a shower, and tomorrow we'll go shopping for your school supplies.'

'Back to normal, right, Mommy?'

'Exactly,' Sharon said, and heaved a sigh of relief. There were no recorded phone messages from Clint, no letters among the mail that had piled up during her absence.

The madness, thank God, had passed.

He knew which day she was due back. The seven weeks he'd spent camping out in a hotel across the street from her prestigious address had allowed him plenty of time to get to know the doorman in her apartment. Extracting snippets of information from the man was a piece of cake for someone with his investigative skills.

He'd spent that particular day reading in the park next door, choosing a spot that gave him a perfect view of the front entrance to her building. He saw the taxi draw up, saw her and Fern get out, and gave her exactly one hour to get herself organised. Then he made his move: twenty yards down the street to the florist's, twenty yards back, and the most boyishly winsome smile he could drum up for the concierge.

'The McClure residence, Charles, please.'

'I'll have to phone up first, sir. I can't let you in otherwise.'

Clint brandished the huge bouquets of roses he carried in each hand. 'I was hoping to surprise the ladies.'

Charles hesitated long enough for Clint to slip him a twenty-dollar bill—no mean feat, considering he was snowed under with flowers. 'Be a good guy and bend the rules just this once. I promise you won't be held responsible if they throw me out on my ear!'

'Very well, Mr Bodine. It's the penthouse lift, at the far end of the lobby.'

It was a very luxurious lobby and a very luxurious lift, so he wasn't unprepared for the quiet elegance of the private foyer when he reached the fortieth floor. Sharon had indeed done very well for herself.

The soft Westminster chimes of the bell had barely faded before Fern opened the door. He couldn't hide the pleasure he felt as her face broke into a dazzling smile of recognition.

'Mr Bodine! I thought you were the pizza man!'

'I hope you're not disappointed,' he teased. 'How are you, Miss McClure?'

'Actually,' she confided, gesturing for him to step inside the apartment with adorable ersatz sophistication, 'I'm supposed to be cleaning my room, which is rather boring, but now that you're here I feel a whole lot better.'

'No more bee-stings to make life exciting?'

She made a face. 'No.'

'Glad to hear it, but I wish you hadn't skipped town so quickly after your last attack. I was going to bring flowers to your bedside, to help you recuperate.

However...' he presented the bouquet of yellow roses with a flourish '...better late than never.'

The sparkle in her eyes would have put emeralds to shame. 'No one ever gave me flowers before!'

He wanted to hug the kid, he really did. That smile of hers touched the most extraordinary soft spot in him, as though he'd known it all his life. 'That's a terrible oversight on someone's part,' he said gravely, and indicated the pink roses he still held. 'These are for your mom. Is she here?'

'Yes, but you can't see her—at least, not right now.'

For the first time, it occurred to him that Sharon might have slipped out by a rear entrance. 'Why not?'

'She's in the shower.'

He ought to have known better than to think for a minute that Sharon would leave Fern alone to fend for herself. Nevertheless, relief left him slightly giddy. 'And I don't suppose she'd like it if I visited her in there, would she?'

The child erupted into an infectious stream of giggles. 'No. She's bare naked!'

Clint's throat ran suddenly dry at the delectability of that mental picture.

'But you can wait till she's dressed,' Fern assured him.

He swallowed. 'I'd like that, if you'll keep me company.'

She looked dubious. 'Well, you'd have to wait till I've finished cleaning my room.'

'Let me help. You'll be finished twice as fast then.'

'I'm supposed to do it by myself—but you could put my suitcases on the top shelf in my closet, if you like,' she decided, her face clearing. 'It's too high for me to reach. Even Mommy has to stand on a chair.'

As she spoke, she led the way down a long hall. The walls were hung with paintings that, unless he missed his mark, were originals, and the marble-tiled floor was covered with a silk carpet runner. Once again, it occurred to him that Sharon had made a tremendous success of her fashion career, if what he had seen of her home so far was anything to go by. He felt better, knowing that. At least not all her ambitions had fallen short of the mark.

'In here,' Fern said, showing him through an open door to a charmingly feminine room.

Peripherally, he noticed the ruffles, the authentic Victorian wicker furniture, but the photograph was what struck him most forcibly. It sat in a silver frame on her bedside table, and he found his eyes drawn to it the minute he set foot over the threshold. It was a typical happy family portrait with Sharon holding Fern on her lap and the late and saintly Jason standing tall and proud behind them.

He'd been a good-looking man, dark-haired and serious, Clint noted sourly. Reliable, stable, all the things he hadn't been when it had been his turn to call her his wife. It was all he could do not to take the damn picture and turn it face down on the glass-topped table.

'That's my daddy.' He hadn't heard Fern approach. She stood beside him, with an armload of T-shirts and socks in danger of spilling over on to the floor, and looked solemnly at the portrait. 'He's dead now.'

'Yes,' Clint said gently, ashamed of himself. 'I know. Your mommy told me. You must miss him very much.'

'I miss having a daddy,' she said pragmatically, 'but I've sort of forgotten what he looked like. I only remember when I look at his picture.'

'I don't remember my father at all, or my mother. They died when I was a baby.'

She regarded him out of large, sympathetic eyes. 'Who changed your diapers, then?'

'My aunts,' he said, laughing. 'You met them at the wedding. They adopted me. Actually, they were my father's aunts, which technically makes them my great-aunts.'

'Oh, I don't have any of those,' Fern informed him, dumping the clothes into an open drawer, 'but I have a grandma and grandpa. They're my mommy's parents.'

'Ah, yes!' Clint leaned against the edge of her desk and folded his arms. 'The worthy Maxine and George Carstairs.'

'How do you know their names?'

'I think your mother mentioned them,' he improvised hastily, and decided he'd have to be more careful of what he let slip, or Sharon would have his head.

'They're my guardians, so they'd probably have to adopt me if something bad happened to Mommy,' Fern volunteered matter-of-factly. 'Grandfather wouldn't mind, but I don't think Grandmother would like it much.'

'Well, not that anything bad's going to happen to your mommy, but why do you think Grandmother wouldn't like it?'

'She says she's always left holding the baby and having to explain it to her friends.'

Clint hid a smile. 'That's just an expression, Fern. It isn't meant to be taken literally.'

'I don't know what "lit..." —what that word means.'

'Well, it means it doesn't really mean what it says.' Then, seeing that his explanation was merely adding to her confusion, he scratched his head and tried again. 'Let me give you another example: if it's pouring with rain, you might say, "it's raining cats and dogs", but you don't actually see cats and dogs falling out of the sky.'

'Don't you like cats and dogs?'

'Yes,' he said, wondering how the conversation had veered so far off the track.

He soon found out that it hadn't. 'Then I still don't know what that word means.' Fern furrowed her brow. 'Because Grandma doesn't like me. She says I'm Mommy's "perpetual reminder", and *that* means I'm a pest.'

And Maxine was obviously still a bitch who hadn't approved of Sharon's second husband any more than she had her first. 'No, it doesn't, sweet pea,' Clint said. 'It means you're an ongoing source of joy and pleasure to your mom and all your friends.'

'You're nice.' Fern's smile was pure sunshine. 'Would you like to see my scrap-book?' she offered, scooping up a large album from her desk and handing it to him. 'I saved every card I ever got, for Christmas and my birthdays and Easter and everything, ever since I was a baby, and pasted them in here—except for these.' She indicated about a dozen loose cards tucked inside the front cover. 'They're the ones I got for my birthday this year, but I haven't got around to putting them in yet. We had to go to Margot's wedding right after my party, and then we went to California.'

Some irregularity in that item of information triggered an objection at the back of his mind—something to do with the timing of her birthday—but before he could bring the anomaly into sharper focus she was dragging her empty suitcase over the floor to the closet.

Stuffing her album under his arm, he went to help. 'As soon as I've stowed this for you, I'd love to look through your scrap-book,' he said, filing the nagging question for later reference. And if he ever ran into Maxine Carstairs again, he'd wring her scrawny neck!

Once the suitcase was stacked away Fern led him into a truly beautiful living-room decorated in shades of celadon and cream and furnished in mahogany. 'You can sit in here; it's more comfortable,' she said, once again the perfect hostess. 'And I'll tell Mommy that you're here.'

'Don't do that.' He settled on a couch and spread the scrap-book before him on a long, marble-topped coffee-table. As he did so, the loose cards that she hadn't had time to paste in place slid out and scattered over the rug at his feet. 'Just tell her she's got company,' he said, bending to retrieve them. 'I want to surprise her.'

Fern giggled conspiratorially. 'I love surprises!'

It took him a few moments to reply. The anomaly was back, distracting him with its insistent demand for attention. 'Don't we all?' he finally murmured, staring at the cards in his hand. Something here definitely didn't add up, and this time the expression meant exactly what it said.

When Fern knocked on her bedroom door and said there was someone to see her, Sharon's first thought was that the pizza delivery boy had arrived early. She wrapped her hair in a towel, turban fashion, belted her terrycloth robe securely, and went down the hall to pay him. But the front door was closed, and the voices—mainly Fern's—were coming from the living-room.

'Please not Mother!' Sharon prayed, moving barefoot across the cool marble tiles. She wasn't in the mood for a lecture on the ill-advisability of pampering a child with extended holidays and junk food.

She was practically across the threshold to the living-room before she realised who her visitor was, and she thought her heart would stop. How often she had dreamed about him in recent weeks; how often she'd woken lonely in the night! But dreams and memories didn't hold a candle to the reality of his presence.

He sat in her pristine living-room, carved like some fallen angel brooding over the loss of paradise in his black shirt and close-fitting black jeans, with his dark gold skin and pale gold hair. She wished she could run into his arms and that the tears suddenly welling in her eyes were inspired by joy instead of grief. Because, of course, no matter what the reason that had brought him to her, she had to send him away again.

'Mommy's here,' Fern said, practically bursting with excitement, and any thoughts Sharon might have entertained about slipping away and declaring herself indisposed for company evaporated as Clint rose from the couch and slowly turned to look at her.

He didn't say a word, just watched her across the width of the room, his eyes veiled, his mouth unsmiling. Fern looked from him to Sharon and back again, that acute radar peculiar to children alerting her to the charged atmosphere. 'Mommy?' she asked uncertainly. 'Aren't you happy that Mr Bodine came to see us?'

Sharon blinked back the tears, 'Yes, sweetheart.' But the answer had a hollow ring, even to her ears, and the air almost crackled as the spool of tension between her and Clint gradually tautened. 'Why don't you go downstairs and visit Jenna now, and leave us by ourselves for a while?'

Jenna was Fern's best friend and lived in the apartment directly below the penthouse. Normally the two girls jumped at the chance to be together, but this time Fern hesitated.

'I thought it would be all right to let him in, Mommy. He's our friend. We know him.'

Clint spoke then, but although the words were directed at Fern his gaze didn't waver from Sharon's face. 'It *was* all right, sweet pea. Your mom just wasn't expecting me, that's all.'

'So I'm not in trouble?'

His face seemed bleached with shock. His eyes, though, glowed like blue coals. 'Not you, honey,' he said, and fired a thin smile Sharon's way. It was the deadliest and most subtle of threats.

Panic skittered over her, leaving her skin clammy and her pulse erratic. Without warning, he moved towards her. She held herself very still, an invisible mist of fear creeping around her ankles and laying icy claim to the blood in her veins.

Clint came to a stop less than a foot away. From a great distance, she heard the front door close behind Fern.

'I've waited seven weeks for this moment,' he said, in a curiously soft, flat voice. 'I think such patience deserves a proper welcome, don't you?'

His hands were cold around her neck. Chillingly so. He stepped closer, tilted up her chin with his thumbs. Her neck snapped back so abruptly that her towel turban came all unravelled and fell to the floor. She went to twist away from him, but he threaded unyielding fingers through the wet tangle of her hair and immobilised her. Before she could object, he brought his mouth down on hers, and his lips were cold, too.

She tried to breathe and couldn't. Tried to swallow, to relieve some of the aching tension in her throat, and couldn't. Tried to close her eyes, and dared not, because his remained open, staring soullessly down at her throughout that interminable, horrible kiss.

'Have you missed me, dear heart?' he whispered, at last releasing her hair and running his mouth over her cheek to her ear.

'Yes.' She was too terrified to lie.

'Then why did you run away from me? After our night together, I thought we were well on the way to a fresh start. Was I wrong?'

'Yes,' she said faintly.

He looked down at her reproachfully and traced the outline of her throat with an icy fingertip. 'Do I take that to mean it was nothing more than a one-night stand for you?'

'No,' she mumbled. She could control nothing—not her brain, not her body. Every part of her, from her voice to her limbs, was shaking. His touch unnerved her completely, left her feeling as though she might disintegrate into a thousand tiny pieces at his feet. 'Please,' she pleaded, 'let me go. I think I'm feeling faint.'

But he was not disposed to show mercy. 'Faint? Oh, I don't think so. I think "frightened" is closer to the truth.' He appraised her face with chilling detachment. 'Why don't we sit down and discuss what it is that has you so petrified of me all of a sudden? Except that...' he backed up to the sofa, leaned against it, and pulled her firmly closer, so that she could feel every well-honed, steely inch of him pressed against her, and he could feel her trembling fear '...it really isn't sudden at all, is it, my darling? You've been afraid of me ever since the day you walked into my arms in the middle of the Dunns' driveway, the week before the wedding. Don't you think it's time you told me why?'

It was the worst kind of nightmare come true, the one where a person could not run from an unseen and oppressive danger. She could not control the shivering apprehension that possessed her. 'I'm cold,' she complained, and that much at least was the truth. But he was burning, she realised, for all that his kiss had chilled her, and although she was moulded against his warmth it couldn't touch her.

'Cold?' His concern was patently phoney. 'Yes, I'd say you're cold. Cold and hard. What other way is there to describe a woman who plays fast and loose with a man's heart, then walks away from him without a word?'

Over his shoulder she saw the roses, at least three dozen lying on the coffee-table on the other side of the sofa, nestled in a bed of maidenhair ferns and tied with satin ribbon. She'd have noticed them sooner if he hadn't blocked her view. 'Is that what this visit is all about, Clint?' she asked, a tiny hope springing to life inside her. 'The fact that we made unplanned love but, this time, I didn't use it as a means of trying to hold you to account?'

'What if I wanted to be held accountable?' he shot back.

If she didn't exactly begin to relax, at least she experienced a slight lessening of the awful tension that had gripped her ever since she'd walked into the room and looked into his eyes. 'I'm sorry if I hurt your feelings,' she said. 'That wasn't my intention.'

'Then let's talk about what you did intend.'

'I'd rather not.' This time when she tried to pull away, he let her go, and she escaped to the piano, because it allowed her to put about as much distance as possible between him and her.

'I'd rather,' he returned inflexibly, 'and, what's more, I think you owe me some sort of explanation. I've come a long way and waited a long time to sort this out, my darling, and I don't intend to be blown off by that sort of excuse.'

He'd never called her 'my darling' in the old days, and the way he kept repeating the words now, with that cutting edge in his husky voice, slashed fine lines through her nerves without leaving a scar.

'So,' he went on, 'why don't you do the socially acceptable thing and offer me a drink? Then we'll sit down together like the nice civilised adults we pride ourselves on being, and you can start at the beginning and tell me exactly what you had in mind when you hopped into the sack with me.'

'That's a degrading and vulgar description, even for you, Clint,' she said, stung.

'I'm a vulgar and degrading man when my pride's on the line,' he replied flatly.

So that was it! She might have known it wasn't his heart that had been hurt.

'Well? Are you going to offer me that drink, or do I pour my own?'

She complied in the sincere hope that, because she did, he'd have the good grace to cut his unannounced visit short. Much more of this cat-and-mouse game he was playing with her emotions, and she'd crack up completely. 'What would you like?'

'Whisky,' he said, his husky voice as unforgiving as an Arctic wind stripping the trees bare, 'and you might as well pour one for yourself while you're at it.'

The fear crawled over her again. 'I never touch hard liquor,' she said righteously, almost tottering to the antique victrola which did duty as a bar.

He stalked her relentlessly. 'Well, believe me when I tell you that, before this night is over, you'll wish you did,' he said, in that same ruthlessly controlled tone. 'Before you and I have finished our little talk, you're going to wish you could swill down anything that will dull your sensibilities as speedily as possible.' He closed in on her until she could feel his breath scorching the back of her neck. 'And after it's over, your life is going to seem like one long, miserable hangover!'

There was a rage in him such as she'd never seen before. It doubled the terror she was struggling so hard to suppress until it threatened to choke her. She had to swallow twice before she managed to articulate a reply. 'You're obviously extremely upset, Clint, but that hardly justifies your ungentlemanly threats. We're talking about only one night, after all, and I'd have thought you'd be glad that, this time, I'm not falling all over you and protesting my undying love.'

His hand reached past her and removed the crystal glass from her grasp. 'You're shaking again,' he observed dispassionately. 'You never used to be so nervous around men.'

'I'm not used to being harassed this way,' she retorted. 'Jason would never have dreamed of treating me like this.'

'Ah, yes, Jason.' Clint raised his drink in a mocking salute. 'Tell me something, dear heart...' He paused, sipped his whisky reflectively, then turned the full force of his chilling blue gaze on her face. 'Did he mind very much taking on a daughter when he married you?'

The blood seemed to ice in her veins. He'd found out! She didn't know how, or when; she just knew. And the only question was what he planned to do with the information. But because a tiny part of her brain held out the hope that she was wrong, that he didn't know or, at worst, only suspected, she had to bluff it out. 'What are you talking about, Clint?'

'The fact that you already had a child when you married Mr Jason McClure.'

'Oh, that!' Agitation left her too light-headed to consider the wisdom of what she said next. 'Your Aunt Jubilee voiced her suspicions to you,' she babbled, 'but that's all they were—suspicions. I'm afraid you've both jumped to the wrong conclusions.'

'Please leave my aunts out of this,' Clint said flatly, sauntering back to the sofa, and retrieving something from the coffee-table. 'And for God's sweet sake, spare me any more of your lies.'

She saw then what lay half concealed by the bouquet of roses: Fern's scrap-book, filled with mementoes of anniversaries, some of which pre-dated Jason's entry into their lives. Clint extracted a card from the heap lying loose on the table, and Sharon recognised it at once. How could she not? She'd given it to Fern herself, an ornate, lace-edged Victorian reproduction of a golden-haired child on a swing under an arbour of flowers. The inscription across the bottom leapt out to indict her: 'Happy Ninth Birthday to a Special Daughter'.

The numbed realisation that the charade had finally played to its conclusion paralysed Sharon and reduced everything to half-speed in somewhat the same way that the truly frightening part of a horror movie slowed down for greater impact. It took the utmost courage for her to raise her eyes and meet the condemnation she knew she'd find in Clint's.

CHAPTER TEN

THE heavy throbbing of Sharon's heart deafened her, battered at her ribs. She clutched at the victrola and felt a fingernail rip down to the quick, but it might have happened to someone else for all that the pain impinged on her. She tried to speak, but although she opened her mouth no sound came out. She simply stood there, stretching her lips like some grotesque gargoyle, while her blood seeped down to her ankles and took every facet of her neatly ordered life with it.

'Don't tell me you haven't got a nice, tidy rebuttal ready,' Clint said. If he had held a knife to her throat with the murderous blade pricking at her skin just enough to draw a pinpoint of blood in a foretaste of what was still to come, she could not have been more terrified.

'I don't—I don't... don't know...' Oh, God, how could she have prepared for this moment? How could she have suspected the pain of trying to explain her convoluted and monstrous deceit?

'You never did lose my baby, did you?' he enquired with deadly composure. 'You just told me that to punish me because I wasn't lavishing you with the sort of attention you'd been used to all your life.'

'I did... lose the baby,' she whimpered.

The ring of Baccarat crystal smashing against mahogany shattered the atmosphere with musical violence. 'What sort of imbecile do you think I am?' Clint raged, contempt blazing in his eyes. 'I can count, Mrs McClure. That's my little girl who sleeps in the room down the hall, and I want to know how.'

He looked lethal. Attila the Hun on a rampage was a pussycat compared to Clint at that moment.

'There were two babies,' she cried on a dry sob. 'I lost one, and Fern...Fern was the twin that survived.'

Her pronouncement effected a miraculous change. His fury died as suddenly as it had flared, replaced by a stunned acceptance of a truth too bizarre to be fabrication. 'You conceived twins?' he asked hollowly.

'Yes,' she said, adding idiotically, 'two of them. Fraternal. I didn't know...not until after you and I...'

He paced around her with about as much trust as a man inspecting a wild cat. 'Why didn't you let me know?'

'I didn't know where you were,' she said, and flinched at the pathetic weakness of such an excuse.

'My aunts could have told you. They always knew where I could be reached.' He lifted a hank of hair from behind and settled a parody of a kiss at the nape of her neck. 'But you didn't want me to know, did you, Sharon?'

She cringed at his touch. 'I didn't...'

He ran stealthy fingers inside the collar of her terrycloth robe, leaving behind a trail of goose-flesh. 'Imagine that,' he said conversationally. 'My oh, so anxious little bride didn't want me to know that I had fathered two children. She didn't want to share any more.'

Suddenly Sharon had had enough. 'How do you know what I did and didn't want, Clint?' she cried, spinning away from him. 'You were no more interested in how I felt then than you are now.'

'Don't you try to turn this around and pin the blame on me,' he shot back.

She ran a distracted hand through her hair. 'I'm not. I'm just trying to make you understand how I felt. I was only nineteen, Clint. A child, divorced and alone. The choices facing me then didn't seem as clean-cut and simple as they might appear now, and if you think any of them were easy you couldn't be more wrong.'

'I'm overcome with pity,' he sneered. 'You poor, misunderstood little thing, having to live with the consequences of your actions!'

'You're not the only one who's suffered, Clint,' she said wearily. 'I know all about loneliness and regret and heartache.'

'You don't know diddly-squat!'

She couldn't look at him, not if she wanted to pursue her own defence. It hurt her too much to see how wounded he was. 'You don't have to forgive me,' she said, her voice catching. 'You don't even have to understand me, but you owe me the chance to explain how——'

'I don't owe you a damned thing, Sharon.' He swung back to the bar and snatched up another glass. She heard the liquor splash over the polished surface of the victrola, heard the decanter crash down on the silver tray, heard his breath heaving in his lungs.

'Even a criminal's entitled to a hearing before he's convicted,' she said. 'Can't you at least allow me that much?'

He tipped back his head and tossed the whisky down his throat in one gulp. Although he stood with his back to her, she could tell from his ramrod-straight spine that he held on to his control by a very precarious thread.

The silence spun out, unbroken, for a good thirty seconds. When he made no move to end it, she took it to mean he was prepared to hear what she had to say. 'You made it very clear,' she began, the truth coming easily at last, 'that you couldn't wait to be free of me. The tragedy of losing our baby was tempered for you by the chance it gave you to get out of a relationship that had never, even at its best, been what you really wanted.'

'I married you,' he cut in rawly. 'That counted for something.'

'Something?' She sighed. 'It counted for everything with me, Clint; that's the whole point.'

'No,' he contradicted. 'If it had, you would have found a way to let me know. You would have wanted that baby to know its father.'

'I did!' she cried passionately. 'I wanted that almost as much as I wanted you to love me.'

'You expect me to swallow that?' His eyes condemned her. 'You gave my daughter to another man, Sharon, gave her another man's name.'

'I didn't marry Jason until over two years after you left,' she said. 'By then I had reconciled myself to never seeing you again.'

'*Two years*? It was more like two months the last time you ran this story by me.' His anger rolled over her like soft thunder. 'Yet not once, in all that time, did it once occur to you that I had a right to know I'd fathered a second child.'

'Why would it?' she flared back. 'You weren't all that thrilled to hear the news the first time around.'

'No, I wasn't, but that doesn't mean I didn't mourn the baby we lost, and you had no right—*no right*, do you hear?—to keep the knowledge of Fern's birth from me. My God...!' He paced to the glass doors leading to the terrace, pounded his fist against the wooden frame and set the panes to rattling, and swung back to point an accusing finger at her. 'You spout off about being entitled to a hearing before I find you guilty, but when did you grant me the same concession, Sharon? Or did you think it was no more than I deserved to wander the face of the earth, trying to exonerate myself for having screwed up your life and, incidentally, my own as well?'

'I didn't think you'd care,' she whispered.

'You didn't *want* to think. It was more comfortable to forget I ever existed. I might as well have been dead.'

'Yes!' She swiped at the tears splashing down her face. 'I told myself you were, because it was easier to get on with my life that way, but I never forgot you, though heaven knows I wish I could have.'

'Well, of course you didn't, dear heart. You had a little reminder in Fern. I can't believe...' he shook his head '...can't believe how stupid I've been. The signs were all there from the start, if I'd chosen to see them. I wonder if, at some gut level, I haven't known all along and just didn't want to believe you'd sink to cheating me like this.' His face was haggard. 'I hope you've found it all very entertaining.'

'I'd hardly call being nineteen and alone and pregnant by a man who disappeared "entertaining".'

'You weren't alone. You had your parents, who were no doubt over the moon that I'd shown myself to be every bit as reprehensible as they'd always thought me to be.'

His assessment wasn't too far off the mark. 'Of course we'll stand by you,' her mother had said, pasting on her martyred air. 'When the time comes, you can count on us to be there.' But when, in the throes of her worst contraction, Sharon had cried out for Clint, her mother had said scornfully, 'Save your energy for what's still to come, Sharon. Clint Bodine isn't going to bring you one iota of comfort or relief, and the sooner you accept that fact, the sooner all this will be over.'

All this... Fern. Love and loneliness. Triumph and sorrow. Victory and loss. Because, despite the joys of motherhood, the success of her career and, eventually, Jason, a tiny piece of Sharon's heart had remained a wilderness—parched, arid, starved. There hadn't been a man alive who could bring it back to life, except Clint. And he had fallen off the edge of the earth.

'Clint...' She appealed to him with outstretched hands.

He shrugged her off. 'Who else knows about this? The whole damned town?'

'Only Margot and my parents—and Jason, of course.'

'I never was quite good enough for the Carstairs' gently reared daughter, was I? Tell me, was Jason more their type? More conservative? More docile?'

'No. He didn't particularly like my mother.'

'Your *father* doesn't particularly like your mother!'

'This isn't about my parents, Clint. It's about us—and Fern.'

'On that, at least, we agree.' He inspected his neatly trimmed fingernails as though it were of the utmost importance that they be flawlessly clean. When he looked at her again, he no longer hid behind anger or cruelty to mask his pain. 'Why couldn't you just have come to me? Or was I too low a life-form, after everything that had happened between us?'

'No!'

He ignored her denial. 'Did I make just one mistake too many—was that it?' He shook his head, his expression mirroring disgust, though for whom she couldn't tell. 'Well, I shouldn't have impregnated you, Sharon. I shouldn't have walked away. I shouldn't have done a lot of things that I did, but you certainly came up with the punishment to fit all my crimes in this lifetime and the next. What I want to know is this: when was it all supposed to stop? If I hadn't come looking for you, would I ever have found out I have a daughter? Or would I have gone to my grave believing I'd ruined your life?'

'Ever since we met again I've wished you knew the truth.'

'Then why didn't you tell me?' The question radiated scorn. 'You had opportunity enough. Our one-night stand would have been the perfect time.'

'No! When you kiss me, touch me, everything else fades away, Clint, even Fern, even the lies. It's always been that way; it always will be. When you make love to me,' she went on, telling him everything now that she had nothing left to lose, 'my whole world becomes you, and nothing else seems to matter. I fall in love with you all over again, so completely that good sense and judgement fly out the window, and all sorts of impossible cravings and improbable dreams fly in.'

He sneered, brushing aside her words with the contempt they no doubt deserved. 'Do you know how long I've blamed myself for our failed marriage? Do you care that there've been other women—*good* women, Sharon, *honest* women—who'd have made excellent wives but who never had the chance because *you* wouldn't vacate the position?'

'You told me none of those women mattered,' she whimpered, aghast all over again at how much it hurt to think of him with someone else. 'And you've never wanted a wife. You're just saying that to punish me.'

'Am I? Haven't you wondered why I showed up here today?'

If she had, she'd long since forgotten. It seemed an aeon ago that she'd stepped out of the shower and into this waking nightmare. 'Why did you?'

'I came to ask you to marry me again.' He laughed with grim amusement. 'I came to ask if you'd let me be Fern's stepfather. Isn't that rich? Now I don't have to do either.'

She ignored his last statement, too amazed to consider its implications. 'Marry me? Why?'

He looked her over as if she were some very good piece of imitation jewellery when what he'd been looking for was the genuine article. 'Because I thought I loved you,' he said hollowly, 'and because I'm such a bloody fool that I thought you loved me back.'

'I've always loved you,' she cried, consumed by pain. 'I never stopped.'

'You expect me to believe that?'

'No more than I believe you,' she conceded. 'Not once, in all the times we've been together, did you tell me you loved me——until now, when it's too late to matter. Perhaps, if you had, I'd have found the courage to tell you what I should have told you nine years ago. Perhaps there wouldn't have been any need to keep Fern a secret to begin with.' She sank on to the nearest chair, dull exhaustion seeping through her. 'Where do we go from here, Clint? It seems there's no repairing the damage.'

'Oh, it hasn't all been a complete waste of energy,' he said. 'I didn't get what I came for, but I'm not exactly leaving empty-handed.' He placed his glass on the mantelpiece. 'I came here a lovesick bachelor and I'm leaving a heart-whole father. Not a bad exchange, I'd say. The only problem is...' his voice faltered, just for a second '...my daughter calls me Mr Bodine, like the well-mannered little girl you've brought her up to be.'

'I never meant it to be this way,' Sharon cried, in a pitiful attempt to exonerate actions grown hideous in the last few minutes.

'You meant to punish me,' he said. 'You meant to make me pay, and God knows I have. Well, now it's your turn.'

A new kind of horror crept over Sharon. 'You can't tell Fern!'

'I can do a lot more than that, my darling. I can sue for visitation rights. I want to get married again, whether or not you're the lucky bride, and I want to make a home. How do you suppose Fern will take to the idea of a stepmother?'

Some other woman supplanting her in her daughter's life? Over her dead body! 'You can take your wife-elect and go to you know where!' she spat.

'To hell, you mean? Oh, I don't think so. I've already spent enough time there to last me the rest of my life. I think I deserve a little bit of heaven for a change. Too bad you won't be the one to share it with me.'

'If you so much as try to drag Fern into a court battle, Clint, I'll make sure you never see her again.'

'Don't adopt that snotty attitude with me, Sharon,' he returned witheringly. 'I won't stand for it.'

'I don't take orders from you, Clint Bodine.'

'As of now, you do. As of now, I'm the one calling the shots.'

Of all the consequences she'd ever imagined, having Fern end up in the middle of a custody battle was the last thing Sharon had ever envisaged. She could think of nothing more disastrous to her daughter's well-being. 'Clint, please! If you have any feelings for Fern at all, don't use her to punish me.'

He surveyed her for a long, long time, his expression unreadable. Then his shoulders slumped and he turned away from her and wandered over to the piano, where there was a photograph of Jason that had been taken just before he died. Sharon kept it there for Fern's sake, because no little girl should have to lose two fathers so early on in her life. 'You really do hold all the cards, don't you, dear heart,' Clint said, 'even to forcing me to play second fiddle to a dead man? Oh, God; oh, God!'

His voice broke and a great shuddering sigh swept over him. When he swung back to face her, she saw there were tears in his blue eyes. She'd never seen him cry. She'd never heard a heart break. She saw and heard both in him at that moment, and nothing she'd ever known hurt her as much as that. She thought the pain might kill her. And wished it would.

'I love you so much.' She took a step towards him, let her whole heart show in her eyes. 'It doesn't have to end this way, Clint.'

He fended her off as if she were poison, and she knew she was about to lose him yet again. 'Stay away from me,' he said hoarsely.

Despair lent her courage. She kept on coming until she could run her hands over his beautiful face and touched her lips to his beautiful mouth. She kissed him, interweaving tenderness with erotic sensuality, employing all the finesse she could muster. It wasn't a role to which she was accustomed, but she couldn't bear to watch him walk out of her life a second time without one last desperate attempt to hold him.

Just for an instant he weakened. For one brief and lovely moment his arms slipped to her waist and his mouth softened in response, before he thrust her roughly away.

'The attraction's still there for us, Clint,' she whispered entreatingly. 'It will always be there.'

'Yes, it's still there,' he acknowledged, 'and it's damned near fatal.'

'You almost kissed me just now.'

'Yes, I did.' His rage was gone, his grief was under control, and he spoke to her kindly, the way a person might speak to an indulged, not very bright child.

Despair withered her heart. 'You cared enough to come here and ask me to marry you. What can I do to make things right for us again?'

He sighed patiently. 'I don't have to explain to you that it takes more than sex to make a marriage work, Sharon. It takes respect and it takes trust. How am I supposed to respect a woman who doesn't trust me enough to let me deal with the truth on my own terms? Tell me that and I might be able to come up with an answer to your question. But in the meantime there's nothing you can do to set things right. I'm afraid this time we really are washed up.'

He was walking towards, the door, out of her life, out of Fern's life. She was ready to grovel, plead, beg... bargain with her life, if she had to. 'Will we hear from you again?'

He misunderstood what she was asking. 'No,' he said, turning to look at her one last time. His eyes were as barren as a wasteland. 'I won't expose your secret—not because I want to spare you, but because of Fern. Because I won't destroy her memories of the only father she's ever known, and I won't show up her mother for the liar that she really is.'

'That wasn't what I meant. I——'

'But in return, there is one thing I do insist on. In the unlikely event that you should find yourself needing financial help—with her education, perhaps, or something like that—I want it to be me you come to, not your parents.'

'I won't know where to find you,' she said dully, a worn-out theme on a broken-down old record.

His lips curled in disgust. 'Try Crescent Creek. My roving days are over, and I'm settling down in my home town. I never got around to telling you that I made a small fortune helping rich families relocate to safe countries. I'm worth rather a lot of money these days—enough to buy the local airport for my private use, and the quarter section next to it. I'm going to become a rancher—inhale the scents and sounds of nature, get back to basics, connect with the environment, and all that sort of wholesome stuff.'

He flung a contemptuous glance around her livingroom, at the baby grand piano, the Persian rugs, the silk upholstery, and shrugged his broad, magnificent shoulders. A rueful smile touched his lips. 'Come to think of it, you probably wouldn't have accepted my marriage proposal once you knew it would mean living in the boonies, even if you did have a private jet at your disposal to get you to wherever you needed to go for your business. I'm afraid Crescent Creek isn't quite up to your impeccable standards.'

She would live with him in a mud hut in the middle of the jungle, but he'd never believe her now. 'Is that all?' she asked, more defeated than she'd ever been in her life.

'Not quite. You can strike your mother as Fern's legal guardian in the event that something should happen to you. I'll take responsibility for my daughter, and, from all accounts, that's one thing Maxine will thank me for.'

He opened the front door, walked into the foyer, pressed the button to summon the lift.

He took her heart with him. She could feel it tear loose and follow him, and the only miracle was that it left behind no visible scar. 'Clint...!' His name strangled on a sob. 'What can I do to prove how much I love you?'

'There's nothing you can do,' he said, stepping inside the lift, 'except stay the hell out of my life.'

The doors whispered shut with their usual well-bred caution, cutting off her last image of him a little bit at a time. And then he was gone and her life was almost the same as it had been two hours before.

Almost, but not quite. Because the burden of deceit had at last been lifted from her shoulders. And because before she only thought she knew what a broken heart felt like, whereas now she knew.

Somehow she got through the next month and a half. School began for Fern, and Sharon worked long hours preparing to show her fall collection, which turned out to be her most successful ever. But the victory was empty and the future bleak. The world of fashion had lost its charm and no longer absorbed her as it once had.

Then, one day towards the end of October, Fern brought matters to a head. 'I heard you crying in bed last night, Mommy.'

'Oh, that! It——' Sharon fumbled for an explanation, but Fern cut her off.

'You cry almost every night, and your eyes are all pink and fat when you get up for breakfast.'

Well, that description certainly fitted! She'd looked like hell in the morning lately, and felt even worse.

'Ever since we got home from California,' Fern went on relentlessly. 'And you get up in the night, too, and make hot milk.'

'I sometimes have trouble sleeping, sweetheart.'

Her daughter regarded her with wise green eyes. 'Then you ought to do something abut it.'

And just like that, Sharon knew that Clint had been wrong. There *was* something she could do to prove how much she loved him. It would take time and it would take courage, and if it backfired it would cost her dearly, but there was something she could do.

'There's something I have to tell you, Fern, and I'm a little afraid,' she said, hoping her daughter's heart would be big enough to forgive the lies and accept the truth. 'It's a secret that I've kept for years, but I think it's time now to share it with you, because it's something you have a right to know.'

CHAPTER ELEVEN

SOME time in the night of December the twenty-third a howling blizzard swept down from the Arctic and blanketed the country around Crescent Creek under almost two feet of snow. Clint stood at the top of the porch steps and looked out at a Christmas-card world, with the trees all draped in white and half the landmarks obliterated. The patches of sky showing between the clouds were the brilliant, intense blue that, this far north of the equator, heralded the onset of a cold snap the likes of which he'd almost forgotten existed. His first Christmas at home in years had dressed itself up royally for the occasion.

They were playing Christmas music on the radio, schmaltzy songs about chestnuts roasting and lovers rolling around in the snow while sleigh bells rang. For some reason it made the ache of missing Sharon worse than usual, a damnable weakness which he deplored but seemed helpless to prevent. He'd tried a thousand times to devise a way back to her, but came up against the same obstacle every time: she hadn't trusted him enough and she hadn't loved him enough. And even having reached that same conclusion every time, still he missed her.

He couldn't rid himself of the memory of that last embrace. The untutored desperation of her kiss had dealt him a fatal blow, but he'd had his sights so firmly set on revenge that she'd slipped past his guard without his noticing it until the damage had been done. He'd been haunted day and night ever since.

They said, those nameless know-it-alls who decreed such lore, that keeping busy helped, so he'd tried keeping busy. He'd built his aunts a smart new bungalow to spare Celeste's arthritic knees and hips. He'd started a thoroughbred horse-breeding ranch on his hundred and sixty acres of rolling land.

He'd also looked for a wife, without success. Not that there weren't willing candidates, even in a town as small as Crescent Creek. As one of the major landowners in the area, plus the fact that he was single and under forty, he was considered extremely eligible. Even Vera Dunn had condescended to invite him to her pre-Christmas soirée last weekend, an event at which he'd been the flattering focus of attention by the cream of Crescent Creek's unmarried ladies. He had tried very hard to drum up some enthusiasm for their regard. Instead he'd been left empty and indifferent.

He ought to have known better. He'd run all over the world for the better part of a decade, trying with a conspicuous lack of success to forget Sharon. She was in his blood, worse than some damned tropical disease, and he might just as well learn to live with the fact.

Behind him, the aunts' old house—his house now—was decked out in winking coloured lights and holly wreaths, in keeping with the spirit of the season. Ever since they'd moved to their new place his aunts had made a habit of sneaking back when he wasn't around and doing things for him, from baking pies to bottling preserves and filling his freezer with three-course dinners that required nothing from him but a quick zap in the microwave oven.

'Because you have no wife,' they'd always say when he asked them why they spent their limited energies on a man perfectly capable of looking after himself. No doubt this latest display of yule-tide excess had been installed for the same reason, and, instead of a winter cruise to the Bahamas, he wished his Christmas gift to them could be the presentation of some suitable woman for their approval as a niece-in-law.

He glanced up at the sky. It was going to snow again. The clouds were thickening into a solid pale grey ceiling, and the temperature had surely dropped another five degrees since he'd first come out of the house. He'd better get a move on if he was to accomplish everything he had planned for the day and be back in time to meet the aunts at the country club for Christmas Eve dinner. There was a stack of paperwork waiting for his attention at the airfield, and before the light faded he wanted to get out to the ranch to check on his prize mare, My Girl. His chief hand had phoned earlier to tell him she'd probably foal before the day was over.

The four-wheel-drive truck slithered briefly on the driveway before cutting a swath through the snow. Across the street a family of boys raced around, pelting each other with snowballs, while their sisters lay on their backs on the ground and flailed their arms up and down to make snow angels.

Clint couldn't help himself. He looked at those carefree kids and, even though he knew the pang would linger all day, he allowed his thoughts to dwell on Fern. What was she doing at this moment? Was she too old to hang up a stocking?

Not that she needed one for the gift he'd be giving to her. The trust fund he'd established in her name would remain his secret, because she was too smart not to wonder why a near-stranger would want to give her the sort of money he intended setting aside for her, and also because he couldn't stomach the thought of receiving a dutiful note of gratitude that began, 'Dear Mr Bodine...' For now, the satisfaction of knowing he was contributing something to her future was thanks enough. He couldn't help but hope, though, that the card he'd sent her would end up another cherished souvenir in her scrap-book.

It was hard to believe that a mild drizzle had been falling in Vancouver and that they were only an hour's flight away from home when they stepped out of the new airport at Harperville shortly after noon on Christmas Eve.

Fern was enchanted. 'I didn't know it would be snowing. It's like Switzerland, Mommy!'

The man in charge of the car rental desk was of a similar, though less enthusiastic opinion. 'Driving thirty miles to Crescent Creek in this, lady? You'd be better to wait out the storm here and go tomorrow. You'll still be in plenty of time for the turkey dinner, and you're more likely to get there in one piece.'

But Sharon was nervous enough at what lay before her. She didn't think she could wait another day to go through with what she had planned. 'I'm an experienced driver,' she assured the man, whose concern was well-meant, 'and surely the ploughs are out already?'

'Probably,' he agreed, 'but at the rate this stuff is coming down the roads'll be clogged again before you know it. However, if you're that determined to go...' He scanned the row of keys hanging on a board behind him and selected one. 'You'd better take something with dual airbags and a good set of winter tyres. I'll get someone to start the engine and warm up the car while you sign the lease.'

It was mid-afternoon before they reached the outskirts of Crescent Creek, but, despite having made slow progress, Sharon didn't experience any real difficulty until she tried to negotiate the long, slow hill that curved up the last half-mile to the aunts' house. The car, which had behaved with exemplary decorum up to that point, balked at the steepness of the grade and slid gracefully backwards, coming to rest with its elegant nose in the air in a drift on the side of the road. Nothing Sharon could do would coax it to move again.

'We'll have to walk the rest of the way,' she told Fern. 'Button up, sweetheart, and put on your mittens. It's snowing again and there's a horrible wind blowing.'

But it was worse than horrible; it was vicious—a freezing gale that numbed their faces and blasted them with snow until they could barely see. Sharon clutched Fern by the hand, knowing that the effort of battling the cold and the deep snow was draining her daughter's strength at an even more alarming rate than it sapped her own.

They weren't dressed for this kind of weather. The gale cut through their clothes as cleanly as a knife through butter, and the final four hundred yards was pure agony. When at last the lights from the house showed through the gloom, Sharon's apprehension at soon seeing Clint again was tempered by huge relief that she and Fern would shortly be warming themselves by a roaring fire.

'Well, we're here,' she panted, pulling Fern into the lee of the garage and out of the worst of the storm. 'Are you sure that you're still up to what comes next?'

Fern swallowed, all her certainty in happy endings apparently swept away in the blizzard. 'What if he doesn't care any more, Mommy?'

'Oh, he cares, sweetheart. No matter how he behaves when he sees me, you can be sure he'll be glad to see you.'

'He has to be glad to see both of us,' Fern insisted.

'I hope he is,' Sharon said, with heartfelt sincerity, 'but even if he isn't I hope you'll still be able to do what we planned.'

Fern looked across at the house. The coloured lights strung along the porch and around the windows twinkled through the gloom in welcome, but Sharon could see that her daughter felt very unsure of herself. 'What if he wants me to stay but he tells you to go away, Mommy?'

'I've booked us a room at the hotel until after Christmas. I'll go there.'

'I don't want to stay here by myself.'

She wasn't nearly as grown-up as she sometimes seemed, and Sharon wondered, not for the first time, if she was asking too much of her daughter. Maybe she'd asked too much ever since that moment in October when she'd decided to try to prove to Clint that she was capable of honesty and deserving of respect, but it was too late to backtrack now. 'The aunts will be there, too. Remember how much you liked them when we came out for the wedding?'

'Yes.' Fern tugged the hood of her jacket more securely around her ears and offered a wan smile. 'Let's go. And don't worry, Mommy. It'll all be OK, you'll see.'

They trudged the last few yards up the path to the steps, with the snow so deep in places that it trickled down inside their boots. Even over so short a distance, the wind slashed at their faces and drew tears from their eyes before they reached the sanctuary of the porch.

'We'd better do something about this, or he'll think we're sorry to see him, instead of the other way around.' Sharon fished through her bag for tissues and stifled the urge to giggle hysterically. She was wound up tighter than a spring, and it wouldn't take much to tip her control over the edge. 'That's better,' she said, mopping at their tears before they froze on their cheeks. 'Ring the bell, sweetheart, and let's get this over with.'

Fern reached for the old-fashioned iron bell and pulled on the handle. They could hear its clanging chimes echoing through the house, but they were the only two who did.

'No one's home.' Sharon sagged with disappointment and fatigue. So much effort, so much anticipation and anxiety, and for what?

'Well, they haven't gone far,' Fern said, rubbing at the frosted window-panes with her mittened hand and pressing her face to the glass. 'They've got lights on down the hall and I can see a Christmas tree in the corner of one of the rooms.'

Her teeth were chattering with the cold, and her face had taken on a pinched, white look that alarmed Sharon. 'We can't hang around out here in weather like this, and it's too far to fight our way back to the car, even if we could get it to go anywhere,' she decided, and groped for the door-handle, half hidden by an enormous beribboned holly wreath.

As was the custom in a town where everyone knew everyone else, the door wasn't locked. It swung open, the tail-ends of the scarlet satin ribbons wafting in the current of warm pine-scented air that streamed out to greet the visitors. 'Come on, Fern,' she urged. 'We'll wait inside and at least be warm.'

There was a fire all set and ready to go in the hearth in the living-room. In the kitchen a tray of freshly baked mince tarts sat cooling on the scrubbed-pine table and a pot of something that smelled like Jubilee's home-made lentil soup simmered on the stove.

Sharon took peripheral note of it all as she knelt and touched a match to the kindling in the fireplace, then turned her attention to stripping off Fern's sodden outer clothing. The child was practically swaying on her feet, and submitted with unusual docility to being undressed like a baby. The cold had eaten through to her bones, and she seemed on the verge of hyperthermia. It was going to take more than the still meagre warmth of the fire to restore her body heat. A hot bath and a bowl of Jubilee's soup were in order.

By the time the grandfather clock in the hall struck four Fern was sound asleep on the living-room sofa, snuggled under one of Celeste's hand-made quilts, and Sharon was left with nothing to do but pace the floor and wait for the aunts to come home and tell her where she could find Clint. But every time she peered through the window it seemed that a bit more of the driveway had been obliterated by the snow, and it occurred to her that perhaps the old dears were stranded and wouldn't make it home that night at all.

By five o'clock her nerves were stretched to breaking-point. She'd waited nearly three months to try to set things right with Clint. She didn't think she could endure waiting another day.

For all her anxiety, however, she didn't hear the sound of an engine or see the lights of a vehicle creeping up the snow-clogged driveway. She was busy feeding the fire, and had no idea that anyone was home until she felt a breath of icy air from the outside weaving around her legs, followed by the sound of snow being stamped from boots too heavy to belong to a woman's foot.

Rising silently from the hearth, Sharon stole out to the hall, half knowing and half dreading that it was Clint who had finally shown up.

He didn't notice her. He slapped the snow from his leather gloves, shouldered the door closed, and leaned against it in a gesture of exhaustion. But if his face was drawn with fatigue, there was an elation in his eyes that more than compensated for it. He was thinner, and he looked not happy exactly, but satisfied and content. Until his glance fell on the two pairs of boots—hers and Fern's—and stared down at them, perplexed and suddenly wary.

It was time to announce herself. 'I wasn't expecting you,' she said, stepping out of the shadows.

He pushed away from the door and flicked on the lamp set on a table near the wall. 'I think that's supposed to be my line,' he said, holding himself very still and wiping his face clean of all emotion. She had no idea whether he was angry, surprised, or shocked. 'How did you get in here, Sharon?'

'The door wasn't locked, and it was so cold outside——'

He rolled his eyes. 'The aunts were here!' he said, as if that explained everything.

'Yes,' Sharon said. 'That's who I was waiting for, but you're not them.'

'No, I'm not,' he agreed. 'My aunts are shorter and fatter. And older.'

'And they're not men.' Oh, lord, Sharon! Better to keep your mouth shut if this is the best you can do!

'To the best of my knowledge, no,' he said, still with that same inscrutable expression. 'Now why don't we stop this silly bantering and you just come right out and tell me what you're doing in my house?'

'*Your* house? But your aunts——?'

'Don't live here any more. They have a new place closer to the centre of town.'

'I had no idea.'

'Why should you? It's hardly any of your concern.' He shrugged out of his shearling-lined jacket and slung it over the newel post at the foot of the spiral staircase. Then he flexed his shoulders and rolled his head in a tight circle to relieve the cramped muscles in the back of his neck. 'What do you want, Sharon? It's been a long day.'

'I can see it has,' she said softly, feasting her eyes on the sight of him. He looked tough and capable, strong, determined and utterly beautiful, but she couldn't tell him so. She couldn't tell him anything of the feelings he aroused in her—how she ached to smooth away the grooves of tension at each side of his mouth, how she longed to go to him and put her arms around him and hold him.

But he must have read all of it on her face, because he turned away and fiddled with the collar of his jacket, as though he couldn't stand to look at her a moment longer. 'My Girl went into labour this morning,' he said, tossing the words over his shoulder like a challenge. 'It's her first, and I feel as if I've been up since dawn. I need something to wake me up, so I'm going to make a pot of coffee. You can join me, if you want, and tell me what it is that's brought you up here in such foul weather.'

She barely heard him. The aunts' absence and the freshly baked mince tarts, the home-made soup, in a house decked out for Christmas with no one home to enjoy any of it, suddenly made a ghastly sort of sense. He was married. His wife—someone else, not her, someone young and fresh and innocent—was about to give birth to his child!

The floor seemed to rock under her, shifting the whole scenario into a new and cruel focus. The chances she'd taken, telling Fern the truth, the hopes she'd nurtured, had all been for nothing. She'd always known they might amount to too little, but she'd never expected they'd come too late. 'Oh, God!'

He jerked around at the sound of that strangled moan, his fear that he might succumb to the grinding need to touch her eclipsed by a more insidious dread. 'Sharon, what's the matter? Is it Fern?'

'Fern?' She looked shattered, her eyes wide and staring, her sudden pallor alarming. 'No,' she said brokenly, 'it's not Fern.'

He reached for her then, afraid she might collapse. 'Tell me,' he begged urgently, and took her hands. They were colder than his, colder than ice. 'What is it? Why are you here?'

The tears gushed from her eyes at that, fountains of them splashing down her face from some deep inner well. She looked small and fragile and beautiful, and he couldn't stand it. It was time to stop fooling himself. His arms, his heart, his whole life, were empty without her.

He curled his hand around her fine narrow waist and drew her to him as naturally as the sun shone on June brides ... and wondered how in hell he'd ever let her go the first time. 'Sharon,' he whispered hoarsely, 'tell me what's wrong and, whatever it is, we'll deal with it together.'

It was the wrong thing to say, though he couldn't fathom why. One minute she was leaning against him as if he were the last solid thing left on earth, the next springing away from him as if he'd stabbed her.

'She might not like that,' she said, her voice bleak behind the tears. 'I wouldn't, in her place.'

'Who?' he asked, mystified. 'Fern?'

'Your... wife.'

She had such difficulty getting the word out that it took him a moment to comprehend what she'd said. Even after he'd figured it out, it still didn't make any sense. 'What wife?' he asked, reaching for her again.

'I'm not married.'

'*Her*, then!' she spat, shying away from him. 'Your pregnant lady or whatever you want to call her.'

Light dawned. He smiled, almost obscenely gratified at the conclusions she'd reached and the reactions they'd provoked. 'You mean My Girl?'

She let out a muffled groan and backed away.

He stalked her. 'My Girl delivered this afternoon, dear heart——'

'Don't call me that! Don't *ever* call me that again!'

'A fine black colt.' He trapped her in the corner, next to the grandfather clock. 'Cute as a bug. You'll love him, dear heart.'

She was all ready to fire another missile of rage when his words sank home and left her speechless. He took immediate advantage and dipped his head to kiss her full on the mouth. She tasted like heaven, and he wondered why he'd been such a stubborn fool that he'd resisted so long something that felt so completely right. 'Merry Christmas, dear heart,' he murmured.

She wrenched her mouth free. 'A horse?' she practically shrieked. 'We're talking about a horse, not a wife?'

'We'd better be,' he said, sliding his hands up her shoulders and imprisoning her face so that he could kiss her again. 'I only met My Girl five months ago, which means she was six months pregnant when I bought her.'

Sharon flushed. 'I've made a fool of myself again.'

'I'm afraid you have,' he said. 'You're always expecting the worst from me, and I can see it's going to take a lifetime to teach you differently.'

Outside the snow batted softly at the windows, insistent as ever, but the frozen look in Sharon's eyes was melting a little. 'A lifetime?' she echoed. 'But you said the last time I saw you that you were going to find some other woman.'

'Some other woman won't do, I'm afraid. A man wants someone who makes him feel like a thirty-year-old lover even when he's eighty-nine and ready to meet his Maker. He wants more than a woman; he wants a wife. A mother for his children. I had both of those things in you, and was foolish enough to let them go. Now I want them back again.'

She looked at him, a trace of doubt in her expression. 'But what about what I did? What about——?'

'No.' He laid a finger over her lips. 'No more raking over the past. What's done is done, and the miracle is that none of it changes the one thing that really matters.'

Her voice trembled, and so did her mouth under his finger. 'What's that?'

'That life with you is better than life without you, and that nothing should keep us apart any longer. I love you,' he said. 'I've always loved you. I always will.'

'Does that mean we have a truce?' she asked.

He reached for her again, threaded gentle fingers through her hair, brought her up hard against him. 'I think "surrender" is more like it.'

'I did that a long time ago, Clint.'

'So did I, dear heart, but I'm only just getting around to admitting it.'

'Are you going to kiss her again?' an interested voice enquired from the shadows of the living-room.

He almost yelped in shock. 'Yes,' he finally managed. 'Merry Christmas, sweet pea.'

'Merry Christmas, Daddy.'

It took a full minute before her answer struck home. It took an answer like that to distract him from the woman quivering in his arms. Not quite daring to believe, he turned to face his daughter. She sat perched on the arm of the sofa like one of Santa's elves, draped in a quilt. The only thing missing was the pointed cap. 'What did you call me?'

'Daddy,' she repeated. 'I hope you don't mind.'

He turned dazed eyes back to Sharon. 'She knows?'

'Yes.'

'You told her?'

'Yes.'

'Why?'

'Because I wanted to give you something special, not just for Christmas but for the rest of your life. Something that I should have given you a long time ago. Something to prove how much I've learned to trust you, and how deeply I've always loved you. I told her everything, Clint, right from the beginning.'

He struggled to find his voice, lodged somewhere at the back of a throat grown thick with emotions he could barely control. 'You didn't have to do that,' he said.

And he meant it. Taking from her wasn't the issue; it was what he had to give that counted. That was what love was really all about.

'Are you going to marry her?' Fern wanted to know, head cocked inquisitively to one side.

'Definitely. I won't take no for an answer.'

'Oh, good! I'll get to be a bridesmaid again.'

'Not so fast, sweet pea,' Clint said. 'This time I have some serious courting to do before the wedding. And there's something you have to do even sooner than that. Before midnight tonight, in fact.'

The first person they saw when they walked through the doors of the country club was Vera Dunn.

'Why, Clinton Bodine, you sly thing!' She intercepted his passage, pouncing on him with the eagerness of a starving coyote. 'I've been looking for you all over the place. I want you to meet my niece, Cassandra.'

'And I want you to meet my fiancée, Sharon,' he replied, drawing them both close to him, 'and my daughter, Fern.'

It was almost worth all the wasted years to see the socially adept Vera Dunn outmanoeuvred on her own turf. She paled visibly and retreated a step. 'You can't possibly mean that,' she declared faintly.

'I was never more serious in my life. Compliments of the season to you all.'

'You enjoyed that!' Sharon accused him, as he swept them towards the dining-room.

He grinned and slid a possessive arm around her waist. 'I did.'

The aunts didn't see Clint and his guests sneak up on them. They were seated with their backs to the room, at a corner table next to the fireplace. Against the window an enormous Noble fir reached to the twelve-foot ceiling, its branches pricked with pin-points of light.

'If Clinton doesn't get here in the next five minutes,' Jubilee boomed, 'I'm going to order another sherry. Will you join me, Sister?'

'Two sherries before dinner?' Celeste sounded scandalised. 'Oh, I don't think so, Jubilee. Why, I might get tipsy and do something foolish like invite the waiter to dance a two-step!'

'Then pray abstain,' Jubilee replied tartly. 'With your feet, you'd look like a duck trying to stamp out a forest fire.'

Fern started to giggle helplessly at that. Shaking a warning finger her way, Clint stepped forward and kissed his aunts on the cheek. 'Make it champagne instead,' he said, 'and we'll join you. This is a special occasion. Merry Christmas, Aunt Jubilee, Aunt Celeste.'

'What sort of special occasion?' Jubilee asked.

Celeste beamed and hugged him. 'Merry Christmas, dear boy.'

'And who's "we"?' Jubilee wanted to know, unmollified. 'I'm not in the mood for guessing games, Clinton. You've kept me waiting too long for my dinner.'

'I have found the perfect Christmas gift for you,' he said.

'Rubbish,' Jubilee declared. 'What you've done is gone out and spent a fortune on things we don't need, when the one thing we'd most like wouldn't cost you a penny.'

'We know you're tired of hearing it, but all we want is to see you get married, dear boy,' Celeste put in.

'I am,' Clint said.

'We're not getting any younger, after all, and it would be nice for us to know that you had a little family of your own before...'

'We're pushing up daisies,' Jubilee finished for her. 'Mercy, Celeste; I sometimes think you can't wait to have me nailed down in my casket, and at this rate it might happen sooner rather than later. Sit down, for pity's sake, Clinton, and read the menu. I'm near starving to death. The gift, whatever it is, can wait until we've eaten.'

Fern started to giggle again, and no number of glares from Sharon could silence her. Neither of the aunts noticed.

Clint sighed and rolled his eyes. 'I said I'm getting married. I'm giving you a niece-in-law for Christmas, one who comes with an extra bonus.'

'I do believe he's serious, Jubilee,' Celeste declared, dropping the menu in her lap.

'There's only ever been one woman for you, Clinton,' Jubilee warned.

'I know,' he said.

Celeste looked behind her then, saw Sharon and Fern, and struggled out of her chair, squealing with well-bred delight. 'Clinton! Oh, my dear, dear boy!'

But Jubilee's head didn't move. She just smiled, a wise, eighty-two-year-old smile. 'So you finally sorted it all out, Clinton, and about time too,' she said, on a satisfied breath, and held a hand over her shoulder. 'Come and give me a kiss, Sharon, and bring my great-great-niece with you. I've waited a long time for this day to come.'

SUMMER SPECIAL!

Four exciting new Romances for the price of three

Each Romance features British heroines and their encounters with dark and desirable Mediterranean men. *Plus, a free Elmlea recipe booklet inside every pack.*

So sit back and enjoy your sumptuous summer reading pack and indulge yourself with the free Elmlea recipe ideas.

Available July 1994   Price £5.70

MILLS & BOON

Available from WH Smith, John Menzies, Volume One, Forbuoys, Martins, Woolworths, Tesco, Asda, Safeway and other paperback stockists. Also available from Mills & Boon Reader Service, FREEPOST, PO Box 236, Croydon, Surrey CR9 9EL. (UK Postage & Packing free)

Full of Eastern Passion...

MILLS & BOON

DESERT DESTINY

TWO COMPELLING AND
PASSIONATE ROMANCES,
SPICED WITH THE MAGIC OF
THE EAST

Savour the romance of the East this summer with
our two full-length compelling Romances,
wrapped together in one exciting volume.

AVAILABLE FROM 29 JULY 1994   PRICED £3.99

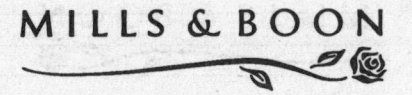

MILLS & BOON

*Available from WH Smith, John Menzies, Volume One, Forbuoys, Martins,
Woolworths, Tesco, Asda, Safeway and other paperback stockists.
Also available from Mills & Boon Reader Service, FREEPOST,
PO Box 236, Croydon, Surrey CR9 9EL. (UK Postage & Packing free)*

Accept 4 FREE Romances and 2 FREE gifts

FROM READER SERVICE

Here's an irresistible invitation from Mills & Boon. Please accept our offer of 4 FREE Romances, a CUDDLY TEDDY and a special MYSTERY GIFT! Then, if you choose, go on to enjoy 6 captivating Romances every month for just £1.90 each, postage and packing FREE. Plus our FREE Newsletter with author news, competitions and much more.

**Send the coupon below to:
Mills & Boon Reader Service,
FREEPOST, PO Box 236,
Croydon, Surrey CR9 9EL.**

NO STAMP REQUIRED

Yes! Please rush me 4 FREE Romances and 2 FREE gifts! Please also reserve me a Reader Service subscription. If I decide to subscribe I can look forward to receiving 6 brand new Romances for just £11.40 each month, post and packing FREE. If I decide not to subscribe I shall write to you within 10 days - I can keep the free books and gifts whatever I choose. I may cancel or suspend my subscription at any time. I am over 18 years of age.

Ms/Mrs/Miss/Mr _____ EP70R

Address _____

_____

Postcode _____ Signature _____

Offer closes 31st October 1994. The right is reserved to refuse an application and change the terms of this offer. One application per household. Offer not valid for current subscribers to this series. Valid in UK and Eire only. Overseas readers please write for details. Southern Africa write to IBS Private Bag X3010, Randburg 2125. You may be mailed with offers from other reputable companies as a result of this application. Please tick box if you would prefer not to receive such offers ☐

mps MAILING PREFERENCE SERVICE